HOUSE
ON FIRE

HOUSE ON FIRE

AUDREY NOTTINGHAM

Tampa, Florida

House on Fire

Published by Gatekeeper Press
7853 Gunn Hwy., Suite 209
Tampa, FL 33626
www.GatekeeperPress.com

This publication is designed to provide accurate and authoritative information in regard to the subject matter covered. It is sold with the understanding that the publisher is not engaged in rendering legal or accounting services. If legal advice or other expert assistance is required, the services of a competent professional person should be sought.

ISBN (paperback): 9781662952975
ISBN (hardback): 9781662952968
eISBN: 9781662952982

Printed in the United States of America

For my husband, Gatz,
my best friend—the one who encourages me
to reach for the stars.
Thank you for supporting me and loving me.
Maybe someday I'll sell enough books
so you can retire and play golf every day.

Love, Audrey

Chapter Now and Then

"**M**Y NAME IS Quinn Thomas, and I am an addict."
I begin each Thursday evening the same at the
Hopeful House on 22nd East Avenue, filled with
lost souls searching for rescue and promise. Or some actually
court-ordered to be here. It has been 2 years and 92 days of
sobriety. Rock bottom landed me with a felony and 734 days
in prison.

This is one of many skeletons in my closet. I drive each
Thursday two hours to tell my story and motivate other fellow
fuck ups. I was born and raised in Beaufort, South Carolina, a
small town filled with southern charm and once even named
"Best Small Southern Town" by *Southern Living* magazine.
Picture-perfect, major motion films setting up post and filming
on the legendary waterfront. "America's Happiest Seaside
Town" they call it. Not for me it wasn't, it was far from picture
perfect.

* * *

Stella, my mother, was vivaciously beautiful. She had long shiny
brown hair with even longer legs. Her complexion was doll-like,
flawless and almost transparent. She always looked well put-

together, even when she didn't leave the house. She reminded me of a TV mom, the ones that wore the silly aprons around the house, and her lipstick never seemed to fade. She was full of energy and personality, and people seemed to be drawn to her, or at least they were before her drinking spiraled out of control. She never quite seemed content with my father, and looking back now it always seemed like she desired a more elaborate existence, like my dad wasn't good enough. For as long as I can remember she never had a real job, although she didn't seem to mind. Now, don't get me wrong, she was extremely intelligent. She earned a bachelor's degree in journalism and was quite a writer before she had me. She would publish small articles in the local newspaper occasionally, but never had the chance to live up to her potential. Her and my dad had met in a bar one night, and after 3 drinks too many, the evening turned into a one-night stand ending in a pregnancy. Stella's writing career was placed on hold, and here I came to wreck her world. I was an only child, an accident, or so I had heard my mother shout more than once at my father.

My father was authentic, and kind, and brave, and I loved him so much. He was a musician at heart who never had the opportunity to make it big, although I believe he would have, eventually. He was talented and learned to play the guitar when he was 8 years old, and then he took a liking to rock and roll music when he was teenager. He was a music teacher by day, and on the weekends, he often traveled to Savannah or Charleston for gigs. Again, he provided Mom with a decent income; however, notably less than the Barlow's, the town's most elite. I inherited the gift of music from my father, and he began teaching me how to play guitar when I was six. After my father passed away, my mother married Brooks, and I was instructed to shelve the guitar because that was not eloquent enough for a little girl gifted with the Barlow reputation. I was forced to play the violin, and surprisingly, I was remarkably excellent at it, and I secretly credited my dad for that gift as well. I was 7 years old when my father was killed in the car wreck, leaving my mother in the arms of Judge Brooks Barlow. That was when everything took a turn for the worse.

Chapter Now

"Q
UINN!" I HEARD the voice of Sherry shouting, the outright most annoying person I currently knew. Sherry runs the Hopeful House and means well, but I was exhausted. The two-hour trip back home I had to endure was irritating enough.

"Yes, Sherry," I shrieked back as I kept walking.

"Wait up. You want to grab dinner? I wanted to talk to you about one of our newbies. I mean, if you have time?" she asked.

Sherry was a recovering meth addict. She had been sober 14 years and started the group 10 years ago, as it was her calling, she alleged. Although I had much respect and admiration for Sherry, she could be taxing. She depended on me more than she should, in my opinion. She was always expecting me to give her insight on newcomers or aid with new groups, and if I lived closer, maybe I would feel more apt to assist. She would also question me a bit more than I think she should have, and she was always checking in on me.

"Sherry, not tonight. I am drained and I have to work in the morning. Maybe next week, okay?" I answered her.

"Sure, it's just he reminds me of you, your stories, I mean. That's all. She . . . well, anyways. Next week, then."

I continued to walk to my car, never turning around to say goodbye. I waved her off and muttered, "Next week, Sherry." The two-hour trip home was interstate, mostly, and I don't know why I moaned about it so much; I did my best thinking alone in my car. I planned my meals, my weekends, my mediations, everything schemed out for the next week on my Thursday-night drives. It was quite productive, actually. I also thought about my dad a lot on the car ride home, and sometimes Miles.

Home was a small studio apartment in Savannah. I relocated to Savannah after I was released from prison. A fresh start, I pretended. No one knew me there, and I could be anyone I wanted to be; well, if they didn't run a background check, anyways. I shared my space with my dog, Sam, whom I knew was chomping at the bit to be let out by this time. Sam always greeted me with a welcoming tail wag, and sadly, he was my best friend, and honestly my only friend besides Sherry. Why was this humorous to me? I still had my sense of humor, shockingly. I had lost a lot, but damn had I held on to that. Truth was, I felt no urgency to make any real friends. Besides, it's difficult to make friends when you're 25 and you literally go nowhere. Bars were obviously out, and nightclubs—well, basically anywhere that young people tended to hang out these days was off limits. I was still debating on church; I wasn't convinced I still believed in God. Maybe someday. I mean, I was optimistic, mostly. I was still "finding myself," or that was my excuse, anyways. Basically, I was scared, terrified of being exposed, and afraid people would figure out who I really was and what I was capable of.

I had gotten a job at a small flower shop. Thankfully, with no background check I was able to disguise myself as a shy, timid girl pursuing a degree in floral design. It was absolute bullshit. I only applied because it was a small, privately owned flower shop unlikely to discover my past. The owner was nice, an older lady that just had a passion for flowers. The shop stayed shockingly busy, mostly with repeat customers and an occasional drifter surprising his love with a dozen roses for their anniversary or an "I'm sorry" bouquet from some douche bag that was caught red-handed. Claudia, my boss, let me go early each Thursday for what she thought was a very exclusive book club meeting, forcing me to randomly read books on the *NYT* bestsellers list. It passed the time when I was home, doing nothing. I had a massive bank account with nothing to spend it on. Sam received an extensive assortment of dog treats each month and had a large stash of the newest and swankiest dog toys. Stella had left the money to me before she killed herself. I didn't work for the money, I worked for stability. And I decided I liked working. I refused to live entirely off my mother's inheritance anyways, so the floral shop it was. Also, I liked Claudia; she was a warm woman who seemed genuine, and she wasn't going to invite me anywhere or try to become a "friend." It was perfect.

Chapter Then

WHEN I WAS 5 years old, I would dream of what most little girls dreamt of: growing up to be a famous pop star and having the most magnificent wedding. I was a cheerful child before my dad passed. I would follow my dad around the house attempting to play the guitar while holding my battery-powered mic. He was my idol. He was gentle and loving, different than my mother. She loved me I think, but in a different way; she was not affectionate like my dad. I would sit in his lap for hours and tell him about what the day had brought, and he always listened intently. These moments were rare, and now, looking back, I remember he was away a lot of the time attempting to get his music career to take off. Most weekends were spent with my mother, but it wasn't until later in life that I questioned whether my mother ever really loved my dad.

*   *   *

On the other end of town was the Barlow family, and unlike us, they came from money. They oozed wealth and high society, and my mother was delighted to inherit the Barlow name after my father passed. She fit like a glove, but I, on the other hand, was a rambunctious little girl, free-spirited like my father, seeming to continually disappoint my mother.

Brooks Barlow had two boys when my mother married him. Brooks was a beast of a man; he towered over me and my mother. For some reason, women found him attractive, and I was convinced it was because of his money and status. He had wavy, jet-black hair and green eyes. He wasn't fit, he was only big in size. If you looked close enough, you could see his belly hanging over his pants even when he stood. His wife had passed away from breast cancer when she was 36, leaving Brooks to raise Kent, who was 6 at the time, and Miles, who was 10. Brooks had an entourage to assist him, his mother Frances being the main one. Frances moved in immediately after his wife's passing to help him with the boys. Brooks married Stella, my mother, less than a year after his wife was buried. Town tea was that my mother and Brooks's love affair began way before they married. It seemed that coincidence was in Stella and Brooks's favor.

I was 8 years old when we moved into Brooks' fortress. Stella had waited about a year before she uprooted me from my safe place. The memories of my dad, the pictures, all his things: gone. I came home from school one day to find a moving truck in our driveway. I had only met Brooks a handful of times, unaware that he was courting my mother. I remember feeling confused and angry at Stella.

That night, after following the moving truck to my new residence, I met my new brothers, Miles and Kent. Kent was younger, an eccentric kid full of mischief and entertainment. He was very welcoming and inviting, but Miles, on the other hand—not so much. Miles was 2 years older than I was, and he was distant. Unlike Kent, Miles was quiet and seemed a bit annoyed that mother and I were invading his domain. Miles was an alluring child, though; jet black hair and dark eyes,

somewhat favoring his father's looks, but managing to bear an innocence about him. I learned that he was a protector almost immediately, because he appeared extra protective over Kent.

I discovered right away that us children were expected to always behave in a certain manner. The family had a prominent status to uphold, and Brooks expected perfection in his presence. Frances made sure we did as we were told, and always to Brooks' standards. I always wondered why Frances stayed, with mother there tending to us. Why they needed Frances there, I never understood. She would often correct my mother, like a mother dog scolding her young. Frances was queen, and mother knew it; accepted it, even. Even at 8, I realized that Frances was a tyrant, the dictator of the Barlow castle, second to Brooks. I mean, 21st century meant nothing to this wicked woman. Stella wanted that lifestyle, at any cost.

I eventually settled in, and most of my belongings were left behind and I was provided with new ones. New bed, new dresser, new clothes, even a new school. I was presented with a whole new identity. I began to attend a private school with the boys, at Brooks' request. Only the privileged attended, and every day after school, Anna, my violin tutor, was waiting. There was a short window before dinner that I was able to escape Barlow reign and Kent and I would explore and play outside, with Miles always lurking in the background. Miles did not interact with me much in the beginning. Kent would run and play with me, building forts in the woods behind the house or making mud pies—for which we were typically reprimanded by Frances. She would shout at us and send us to the bathroom to wash off the rubbish.

Miles was intelligent, a genius, apparently ahead of most, and he had even skipped a grade. He was a no-nonsense type. He would follow Kent around, hovering, and it puzzled me.

Why even trail us if you don't want to participate in our antics?
It was not until about a year later I figured out why.

Things were different in that house, my mother especially.
The outspoken and confident woman I had known before
began to fade quite quickly. She had begun drinking heavily
and slept a lot. I rarely heard Stella and Brooks argue, which
was unusual with Stella, because she'd never kept her mouth
shut with my dad. Mother was now submissive and weak, and
I began to imagine she was nothing but a robot on autopilot.
Strangely, she and Brooks were somewhat affectionate at
times, which was surprising, although she was never warm
towards me. I assumed she was loving towards him because he
commanded it. I envied him at times, wishing I could crawl
onto her lap and hold her like I used to with my dad. I missed
my dad every single day, but I dared not mention my father,
especially around Brooks. Brooks was a lot like my mother—
distant and non-affectionate towards the boys. I never saw him
hold them or even hug them.

Every night following dinner, us children were expected to
disperse to our rooms and stay there until morning. It was odd,
but not bad. Until it was . . .

Chapter Now

S AM WOKE ME up. *Who needs an alarm clock when I have you, Sam?* He licked my face, pleading with me to take him outside. Before rolling out of bed to oblige Sam, I scrolled through my phone. Keeping up with the current events was my new thing. It entertained me to some extent, and most of it was nonsense, nothing worth reading, but it sufficed and passed the time. One headline caught my eye that morning: *Human remains reportedly found along Albergotti Creek.* I read on as it alleged that two hikers stumbled upon human remains in a remote location near a creek bank in Beaufort, SC, according to Sherriff Kent Barlow.

I read on. Kent was only 23 years old and had become sheriff less than a year ago. He was a shoe-in. His father's reputation was outstanding with the citizens of Beaufort, and he was elected by a landslide. Home-cured gentleman with his daddy's passion for justice. I could not continue reading, the shock was so pressing. My body felt numb, and I began to feel nauseated. *Have they found him? Have they found his body?* All I could think about was Kent. My heart ached; I prayed it wasn't so. I loved Kent, even still. I hadn't talked to Kent since I fled several years ago, and he loved his father; after all, he never endured the torture Miles and I had. I wasn't even sure he knew what was going on in that house. He had been young and naive. In that moment I wished I could call Miles; I needed him to comfort me and tell me everything would be okay, but I had no idea where he was.

*   *   *

Judge Barlow had disappeared 9 years ago, shocking the flawless, crimeless town of Beaufort. Gone without a trace, never to be heard from again.

I couldn't think about that right now; I needed to take Sam out and get to work. I stared at the new me in the mirror, unimpressed. I was lanky and pale, reminding myself of the old me in that instant. *You're doing a terrible job of re-forming yourself, Quinn.* But I'm sober, so there's that, I argued with myself, again snickering that I indeed still had my sense of humor. I did have the potential to be attractive, but I was afraid to invest in myself, like I didn't deserve it. I took Sam out, dressed for work in a flash, and headed out the door like usual, still lanky and pale.

On the way to work, the article relentlessly prodded at me. It was drudging up memories, things I had fought so hard to forget, things I was still fighting every day to overcome, and not just the horrific memories, but the temptation to seek escape. I arrived at the flower shop and Claudia had beaten me there, already starting without me. I made my way to the back and threw on my apron. I looked at my watch, checking the time to be sure I wasn't late, and I wasn't. I grabbed the order sheet, and all the while, I was unable to stop thinking about the article, feeling worried and a bit dazed. I could really use a hit right now, I thought. My hands even felt unsteady.

"Good morning, Quinn. We have 3 orders for delivery uptown." She paused. "Is everything okay? You seem a bit . . .

off, today," Claudia stated as she stared at me in polite concern. "And you look pale. Are you feeling alright?" she asked.

"Yes, I'm sorry, yes, I'm fine. I'll get on those orders now. Thanks." I returned a forced smile back at her. It was obvious I was preoccupied, even for Claudia, my 70-something-year-old boss. She nodded her head suspiciously while grabbing a small pot and heading back to the storefront.

All I could think about were the remains found. *Could it be Brooks Barlow after all this time*? I wondered. I began to work on my orders, a fresh bouquet of classic all white flowers. I recklessly began cutting the stems, slicing my finger rather deeply while doing so. Blood made me queasy, and it began to gush . . . I fell to the ground, sending a thud echoing through the shop. A flashback of Brooks lying there in a pool of blood had done me in, and down I went. I woke up to Claudia kneeling beside me, rubbing my hair out of my face, shouting on her cell. She had called the ambulance. She was repeatedly asking me if I was okay. My head was throbbing. I evidently had hit my head, and her shouting was only intensifying the pain of my now aching brain.

I was unable to convince the paramedics that I did not need an ER visit, and Claudia also kept insisting that I go. My finger needed stitches and I had what felt like a baseball on the back of my head, so I complied.

As I arrived at the emergency room, it was crowded, little old ladies sitting around and babies crying. The ER also succeeded in recalling more terrible histories of the old me. The day just kept getting better.

I had spent many evenings in ERs, begging for oxy or Percocet, or whatever they were willing to hand out. I had a half a mind to up and leave, but my finger was in desperate need of some attention. The paramedic had wrapped it up so tight it was throbbing, but it was no longer pouring blood. *I could probably super glue it*? As I was considering hopping out of the unpleasant hospital bed, more of a cot really, the nurse walked in. "Quinn Thomas?" she asked.

"That's me," I countered as I sat up. As I rambled on to her about what happened, I cut my finger blah blah blah, she began to unwrap my finger and clean it. The nurse poured some cleaning solution on it, making it sting brutally. As I shouted the word "SHIT!" rather loudly, I could see a man enter in the corner of my eye, wearing a white coat. The nurse ceased cleaning and caring for the cut to hold my finger up in the air, as if presenting it on a platter. I shut my eyes temporarily, the wound making me feel slightly sickened and lightheaded again. The nurse then spoke to the man in the white coat. "Dr. Barlow, it's a harsh cut from small gardening shears. I have it cleaned up. Let me go and grab the supplies. Miss Thomas, are you allergic to anything? Can I get you something for pain?" she asked as she headed towards the door. *Please God yes.* But I knew better. "No, thank you, I am good," I replied as I looked up to see Miles standing 3 feet from me. It was him. *Were my eyes and ears deceiving me*? I froze and gawked; the pain vanished in an instant.

He came closer, standing over me as the nurse reappeared setting some gauze and things on the bedside table before leaving again. Miles had the strangest look on his face. I couldn't read the peculiar look. As the nurse left the room again, he continued to stand over me, staring with intense eye contact. "Quinn," he finally said in a tender voice. My hands and body began to tremble. I had not seen or spoken to Miles in years. He had left me there alone to deal with what we had done. I felt terribly confused, unsure if I was elated to see him or resentful.

The nurse returned to the room, abruptly handing more supplies to Miles. Miles took a seat quietly beside my cot and began to deal with my finger. The nurse had rolled over a computer and began to ask me questions. The normal routine, I supposed. It was a suitable diversion, considering the awkwardness I felt between Miles and me. We had never spoken about that night, had never had the chance to speak about the night that changed everything. So many things were left unsaid, but I was working so hard on coming to terms with the reckoning, and now here I was, face-to-face with him, my history.

As he stitched up my finger, I wondered. Wondered what he knew about me, wondered if he knew what a disappointment I had become. *Did I ever cross his mind?* He was beautiful, just as I remembered. He was taller, defined and muscular. His hair was still jet black, with the most stunning eyes. His skin was flawless, and his jaw could cut glass. He had definitely taken better care of himself than I had. I could feel my face blush; I was embarrassed. I was clearly not prepared to run into the former love of my life today.

Did he know they found a body? I had so many questions. The questions consuming my brain were making me feel sluggish. He wasn't wearing a ring, but there was no way this man was single. I immediately regretted my choice of attire for the day. I had on a baggy shirt with leggings, and after the morning I had, I had neglected to put my face on. I was tall and thin and pale, as Claudia had pointed out that morning. Nothing to look at. I had long brown hair, slightly wavy, with hazel eyes. I had never colored my hair. Stella used to refer to the color as mousy brown, always pressuring me to do more with it. I probably would have, had she not demanded that I did. Anything to go against the grain or the authority of that house.

"Looks like we have that finger all fixed up," Miles timidly stated as he stood from his seat to wash his hands. Miles looked at the nurse and told her radiology would be coming in soon to take me for a CT scan of my head. The nurse and Miles examined the knot on my head and Miles performed some neuro tests on me, which was completely and utterly uncomfortable. I could smell him, and it made me weak. I had always been fond of his natural smell. He stopped at the door with the nurse, never looking back at me. They chatted briefly, and he walked out the door.

Chapter Now

I DID NOT SEE Miles again before being discharged. Claudia had followed the ambulance and was generous enough to take me back to my car. She demanded she take me home, but I declined; I wanted my car. I convinced her I required it in case I needed to revisit the ER for some reason. By this time, it was after 7, and I desperately needed to get home to let Sam out. My studio was on the top floor of a small building downtown. It was nice, and nothing I would have been able to afford without Stella's money, but I persuaded myself that it was my base. I spent the majority of my time there, and I wanted an appropriate environment for my *new life*. Really, I had spent 2 years in a jail cell with basically nothing, and it was my reward for sobering up. After Brooks disappeared and my mother died, I inherited her part of his fortune, and of course her life insurance, or a third of it anyways. I was left out of his will; however, mother left me as beneficiary of a hefty life insurance policy along with what Brooks had willed her. She outsmarted him for once. Francis had passed away, unable to contest, although I believe she would have.

As I shuffled out of my elevator, I spotted Miles. He was sitting on the floor in the hallway with his back against my door. I could hear Sam barking faintly as I approached the door. He stood up facing me, wordless. I felt my body stiffen up as he stood there in front of me. I was staring angrily into his eyes. I had so much to say but my brain could not persuade my mouth to say it. So instead, I reached inside my purse to search for my keys. He grabbed my hands, gesturing to me to stop.

"How do you know where I live, Miles?" I asked curtly as I unlocked my hands from his grip.

"I looked in your chart. I hope that's okay. Had no idea you were living here in Savannah," he responded. My head began throbbing, banging like a 1st grader playing with his first drum set.

"Yeah, I guess you wouldn't, would you?" I shot back as I unlocked my door.

Sam was now scratching on the door. I knew he could hear me outside. He always throws me a small party when I arrive home, and most days I found it gratifying. Today was different. I was aggravated and puzzled. *Why in the hell is he here now?* He must have heard about the remains found on the creek bank in Beaufort from Kent, because he sure didn't seem to care earlier at the ER, at least about my existence, anyways.

Miles didn't reply to my comment. He stood tall there in the hallway, now with his hands in his pockets. He was hard not to stare at, as a perfectly built human and a physician now. Out saving the world, saving addicts like me. I was admittedly somewhat intimidated by his presence.

"Can I come in?" he asked.

I waved him in as I bent over to greet Sam. "This is Sam."

"Hello Sam," he said as he rubbed the top of Sam's head.

Some guard dog you are, Sam. He didn't know a stranger, it seemed. Although I never had company, he was always friendly to the neighbors on our trips outside.

I put my purse and the hospital papers down on the table. "What are you doing here now?" I questioned him. Miles ignored my question and began surveying my place. He walked into my living room examining my possessions. "Can we sit?" he requested. "No, we cannot, but you're welcome to walk back downstairs with me. I have to take Sam out," I stated with authority. I knew Miles too well, and he appeared much tougher than he really was. He was the kindest, most gentle person I had ever known. Or at least that's how I remembered him. "Take off the boxing gloves and relax. I'm not here to upset you, Quinn," Miles stated as we headed downstairs. He in fact did not know about the whole human remains situation, and it was a jolt. I thought he may puke right there in the parking lot. I wasn't sure if he was worried about Kent or the truth coming out. I didn't dare ask. Seeing Miles felt surreal. For so long I had yearned for him, missed him, and then that ache had turned to bitterness. It was easier to be outraged at him for ditching me. I blamed him for my addiction, for what I had become. Now, seeing him fueled that fury. He had succeeded after he left me. I mean, clearly he had made something of himself, and everything had worked out just fine for him.

I reluctantly agreed to meet Miles for dinner the next evening. I wanted to be courageous and make a stand by denying his request, but I folded. Miles, as angry as I was at him, was still the one that got away. I had secretly remained hopeful that someday I would see him again, and here he was. And although the secret we kept did bind us forever, there was more to us than that tragic night.

That night I barely slept. With Sam at my side, I tossed and turned most of the night. I reminisced about the good times along with the terrible. Claudia had graciously given me a few days off, and it could not have come at a better time. I really needed to concentrate on staying healthy and to prod into what was happening in Beaufort. I had failed to ask Miles if he spoke with his brother regularly. I imagined he did, which didn't make sense to me. He left me behind; did he leave Kent as well? I had so many questions I wish I had asked him before he left the parking lot that evening. I was overwhelmed emotionally and never found the nerve. I would get my chance tomorrow night at dinner.

Chapter Then

A FTER I SETTLED into my new existence, I buried myself in the violin. I felt close to my dad when I played. He was so beautifully talented when it came to music, and I had no choice but to embrace my new sanction. I liked Anna, my instructor, because she was pleasant and loving. She would chat with me about school and even sneak chocolate or candy to me occasionally, warning me not to tell. Anna was 22 when I met her. She had graced many famed concerts all over the world, only to return home to care for her dying mother. She was remarkable, and she was patient with me. If it weren't for Anna, I would have strayed long before I did. Anna asked me frequently if I was alright. She asked a lot of questions about Miles and Kent, and it confused me. I did not understand her concern, until I did.

One evening, after being sent to my room after dinner, I did it. I defied the rules of Brooks and Frances, and I left my room. Mom had been on a binger that week and had spent most of the day hidden away in her bedroom. I tiptoed down the hallway planning on coercing Kent to sneak into the kitchen with me for a brownie. I was 9 years old at the time. I made my way to Kent's room and gently tapped his door before

attempting to open it. It was locked. I whispered his name and
told him to open up, but there was silence; he never answered
me. I lost my nerve to go downstairs alone, so I crept down to
Miles's room to plead with him. His door was shut, and as I
turned the knob, it opened. I found Miles sitting on the floor
at the end of his bed holding his knees to his chest, weeping
silently. Miles looked up at me with desperate eyes, as the tears
kept rolling down his cheeks. He said nothing. He pressed one
finger to his lip gesturing to me to be silent. He then pointed
to the door requesting me to leave. I made my way back to
my bedroom, as I had lost my nerve and my appetite. I would
not go down to the kitchen that night. Instead, I lay in bed
contemplating why Miles was sobbing. To my knowledge,
Miles was not even capable of crying, he was so serious.
Never vulnerable or fragile, he always presented so tough at
that time.

The next day I confided in Anna, "He was crying. I've never
seen him that way."

"Quinn, listen to me. Do as you're told. I mean it." She spoke
with a face gripped by sheer terror. She cuddled me tight and
told me she loved me that day. We ended up skipping rehearsal
that day and caught up on the school drama happenings. I was
not allowed to have friends over, nor was I allowed to visit
other friends' residences, another one of Brooks's ridiculous
rules. Anna was my only friend.

After "practice" that day, Kent and I had decided to play
out back on the swing set. Kent was his regular, playful self,
swinging entirely too high, giving Miles what appeared to be
a slight panic attack. He hollered at him to be careful. Miles
wouldn't even look at me that evening, I presumed out of
embarrassment. I did after all catch him bawling like a girl
in his room the night before. I recall Frances called from the
back door summoning us to dinner that evening. We obeyed

and cleaned up for dinner as instructed. But that evening was different, mute around the table. A feeling of doom surrounded me. Brooks was visibly agitated and upset, and no one dared speak. His face was flushed, and his eye appeared darker than normal, and mother had managed to make it to dinner but looked as if she had been crying. She never looked at me once during the meal, and it made me uneasy. As usual, dessert was served, and we were then excused from the table to our rooms. As I wandered to my room to shower, I heard footsteps pursuing me, ringing heavily, sounding intimidating. I hurried to my room and shut my door. I was a few steps into my room as my door swung open. Brooks was standing there in my doorway, glaring at me. He was about 6'2", and his silence was terrifying. He typically had a daunting disposition, but tonight he looked evil, and I was instantaneously frightened. He rarely spoke to me, only occasionally asking me to play my violin, which I figured was to make sure I was progressing. As he stood tall, I held motionless, anticipating a conversation. Except there was no conversation. He removed his belt and grabbed my hair, thrashing me around onto the edge of the bed. He whipped me four times across my rear, each one aching me to the core. He then snatched me up as I wept and signaled to me to go to my bathroom. As I stood there in the bathroom, he uttered only one sentence to me: "Do as you are told." He slammed the door to my bathroom and exited the room. I heard his footsteps fade, bringing me some relief. I was baffled in that moment; my only thought was Miles had snitched on me for leaving my room. It was a prison, Brooks was the warden, a harsh certainty that became clear that night. My mother never came up that evening to say goodnight, that pained me more than the beating itself. I was not allowed a phone, otherwise I would have called Anna to say *come get me please*.

The next morning, I woke. I dreamt of my dad that night. The thought of him always seemed to bring me peace. As I turned the doorknob to go downstairs for breakfast, I found it to be locked, but not from the inside. I spent 4 days inside that room, alone and terrified.

Chapter **Now**

THE FOLLOWING DAY, I devoted considerable time to researching details about the human remains discovered in Beaufort, with thoughts of Miles and Kent frequently occupying my mind. With no luck, I found nothing more than I already knew, which was not much. I was anticipating my dinner with Miles, but human interaction was not my strong suit these days. I had become very good at shielding myself from having or feeling emotion. I discovered long ago vulnerability was a weakness. If I don't feel it, it can't hurt me. With Miles I knew this would be difficult. And to be honest, I wasn't sure how I felt about him anymore. I was still angry with him, but seeing him in the flesh felt so invigorating.

Why am I so worried about my outfit? I found myself longing for a friend to walk through my closet with to help me select an outfit. *It's a depressing closet*, I thought, literally 4 pairs of jeans and 12 pairs of joggers. It was slim pickings, for sure. I was never the shopping type of gal, but tonight I wish I had been. This was my fault. I had managed to dodge every potential friendship tossed my way. I met several appealing personalities from the Hopeful House, many summoning a relationship; however, I did what I could by pushing them away and refusing to let them in. Brooks had shattered my ability to trust anyone fully, and all I saw were flaws in people. I was responsible for the seclusion and the lack of connections or friendships. Tonight, though—this was a big night for me. I planned on confronting Miles with my questions and my feelings . . . Well, maybe.

I chose a pair of high-rise jeans, one of the 4 pairs hanging in the closet, and a simple nude sweater. I had no dress shoes, only an old pair of black-and-white Vans and a pair of black closed-toe flats. I chose the flats, the flats which had only escorted me to my job interviews in the past. We had agreed to meet at a restaurant close to my home downtown. I had never been, but reading the reviews, I was surprisingly enthusiastic. Italian food sounded incredible, considering the closest thing to Italian food I had in years was a Digiorno pizza in my oven. I was uncomfortable in society amongst others, my age especially, and it was intimidating. I was never chic or popular anyways, but being incarcerated didn't help the whole self-esteem issue I had going on. Of course, that hadn't been the cause of my self-isolation; that was the temptation, the craving of alcohol, which always led to the pills or the lines. I spent most of my time reading, meditating, or studying music while locked up— or thinking about Miles and Kent. Miles was a doctor now. So impressive. He was always a smart and determined child. It shouldn't have shocked me. His need to protect or heal others came so naturally to him. He was always following us around making sure we were careful and unscathed, Kent mostly. He was so gentle with him; he would run and grab the peroxide and a band aid when Kent would scrape a knee or an elbow. And after him and I grew close, he would always make sure I felt fancied and loved. He would hug me for no reason or offer to help me with my homework, all while dealing with Brooks abusing us both behind the scenes.

I arrived at the restaurant before Miles. My nerves were shot. I bit my nails down to the cuticle. Not an attractive look. I sat there impatiently waiting for his arrival. He walked in about 10 minutes after me, but still 10 minutes early. He wore jeans, thankfully, and a red collared shirt. He was casual, which eased my mind to some extent. I weirdly stood when he arrived, then delayed hugging him. It was an uneasy moment for sure, and I felt embarrassed, assuming he noticed my overwhelming anxiety. I could feel the sweat pooling in my palms, and I was certain my face was faint. It felt like my blood was draining out of my body right there in the restaurant. He embraced me tightly anyways for what felt like 5 minutes, saying nothing. Time and pain had separated us, but I felt so secure with his arms around me. "Retrouvaille," I blurted out awkwardly. I pulled away from him suddenly and began to define the word I had just blurted out.

"Quinn, I know what Retrouvaille means."

Of course he did, I secretly thought. I had read the dictionary twice while in prison.

"I don't know why I said that," I stated as my face went from pale to red in a flash. I sat down, and he followed suit. He attempted to push my chair back in for me but instead I scooted it up in a hurry before he could. I hid my hands under the table, insecure about the damage I had previously done to my nails, and not to mention my sweaty palms.

"It is indeed a reunion; I suppose that is why you said it," he finally spoke as he sat. "Quinn, I don't even know where to begin," he said as he placed his napkin in his lap, all while holding eye contact with me.

"Have you talked to Kent? I mean, do you talk to your brother?" I blurted out once again. He failed to answer the question by diverting to the menu.

"I hear they have amazing lasagna," he responded as he began to explore the menu.

"Miles, why did you ask me here?" I demanded. I needed him to sincerely apologize and beg for forgiveness, for him to say I've missed you. He didn't plead for forgiveness. Instead, he made small talk, beginning with, "How have you been, Quinney?"

Chapter **Then**

JUDGE BROOKS WAS a well-known and well-loved judge in
our community. Stella was forced to host posh parties and
exclusive events. Our home was enormous, with space to
accommodate. Frances would tend to us children while mother
and Brooks charmed the party goers. From the outside, we
looked like an ideal, all-American family making impeccable
decisions, from our grades to our behaviors, all holding notable
talents. Kent was an athlete, always the quarterback, and
Miles was a wunderkind, valedictorian of every class he had
ever been in. Then there was me, petite and well-mannered, a
musical genius, displaying my violin abilities at many parties.
Unsuspecting visitors were unaware of what was really taking
place inside those walls. Even then, at school, I would deny
friendships, knowing that I would never be able to truly invite
someone inside my confinement.

I was desolate.

Anna never returned after I was summoned to 4 days in my
room. At some point, after the initial incident with Brooks,
Miles warmed up to me, each day growing closer. I was now
one of them. Mother was in denial, or at least I told myself
she was ignorant of what was occurring. Looking back, I was

the one in denial. Stella allowed him to beat me, to hold me to an unobtainable standard. I eventually recognized he was also hurting her. She would try and cover the bruises, but we noticed them. He was cautious. He knew when and where to strike. I always knew when it was really bad. Brooks would whisk her off on a trip, buying her reconciliation. She would return to a house full of flowers and melt like butter into his arms. She would willfully pardon him every time.

Brooks never hurt Kent, or so we believed. The lashings were directed at Miles and me, and mother of course. Miles and I never held it against Kent. He was the fortunate one. As Kent became older, we believed he knew and seemed somewhat sympathetic. He loved Miles, and he loved me. But he was the golden child in Brooks's eyes. He was always praised by his father, and they seemed to have somewhat of a normal bond. Kent was caught in the middle, and it wasn't his fault. By high school, Miles and I were inseparable. I found myself thinking of him throughout every day. He was so kind, so defensive. He would occasionally interject and smash through my door, shouting at Brooks and pulling him off of me. Knowing the consequences for doing so never stopped him. I became stronger as I grew older, able to fight him off at times. It was easier to fight off Brooks when he was in the brown water. He would become sloppy with slow reflexes. Sometimes he would lock the door, and I could hear Miles at the door demanding him to stop. Brooks took pleasure in assaulting me. He would tell me I asked for it. He would call me a tease and a whore. The sexual mistreatment did not begin until I was 14. Before that, he only slapped me around, and sometimes for absolutely no reason. When I say slapped around, I'm utilizing that term lightly; it was extreme, resulting in numerous trips to the emergency room explaining to the staff about how I slipped on the stairs and hit my face on the handrail. I expected the usual beatings for spilling a glass or not taking off my shoes before entering or showing up last to the dinner table: those thrashings I could prepare for. It was the unprovoked attacks that hurt the worst. When I was 14, that's when I certainly labeled him as a monster. The emergency room staff never assumed the worst. It was, after all, Judge Brooks Barlow, the friendliest man in town. A righteous, caring man with great family values. Upstanding civilian reelected time after time. No one questioned it, or at least at the time that's what I understood.

Miles and I never talked about the sexual abuse. I was embarrassed, and I nearly believed that I deserved it. Brooks convinced me that I did, and I felt ashamed. My mother, Stella, never once asked me about it or consoled me. No doubt she could hear Miles pounding on my door screaming at him. Frances also turned a blind eye to all of it. Brooks was Frances's golden child, even still.

By high school I managed to get a phone. Anna had visited me at school, bringing me a cell for emergencies. We would keep in touch just about daily. Her mother eventually passed away, and she relocated to London to instruct at the Violin Institute. I was grateful she managed to keep in touch, but eventually she met a gentleman, and her phone calls became less frequent. I never faulted her. I understood that she was busy building her own life. Me, I was trying to survive, attempting to appear normal to the outside world. It was exhausting. I had a particular tree out back in the thickets that I would visit every day after school. It was a sycamore tree, and it stood about 60 feet tall, near the stream at the end of the property line. It towered above the other trees, never giving in to the attacks from the weather or the fungus invading the other trees surrounding it. This tree was different, solid and impressive. I would sit underneath it for hours if I were able, watching the branches dance in the wind and listening to the leaves rustle in the breeze. It was calming, reassuring, reminding me of my dad. Miles kissed me for the first time underneath that tree. That tree had witnessed many tears.

Chapter Now

How HAD *I been?* I wondered if he wanted transparency, although I knew I wouldn't give it to him. I realized I wasn't prepared to answer his questions, only to ask the questions.

"Can we not do this, Miles?" I asked as I peered directly at him with annoyed eyes. The waitress had now appeared at the table asking if we were ready to order. She handed us both cocktail menus, genuinely apologizing that she was unaware that we had been seated.

"Just water for me, please," I responded, handing the cocktail menu right back to her.

Miles paused and looked over at me. "Nothing from the wine menu? I will share a bottle if you'd like. White or red?" he asked.

"No thank you," I stated firmly as I felt myself becoming more and more impatient.

Miles ordered a glass of pinot grigio and a pesto dish. *Of course he did,* I thought. What an experienced pairing. He and I had come to know a lot, lingering about the lavish parties held in our home growing up. Hell, I was nearly a wine connoisseur myself. Francis would brief us children frequently to be sure we did not embarrass Brooks amongst company. I didn't care about chardonnay when I was 11 years old, but we mustn't appear ignorant while we were fetching drinks or fraternizing with the fancy folk.

"Have you spoken to Kent? And can we please just skip the whole part where you pretend to be interested in how and where I have been the last 8 years?" I expressed with haste. I was still debating internally how I felt sitting across from the one whom I believed to be my soul mate once upon a time.

"Don't do that, Quinn," he said as he threw his napkin from his lap onto the table. I could tell I had finally frustrated him. "I left Kent a message. He isn't the best at returning my calls," he said as his phone began to buzz. "Let me grab this," he said as he stood and removed his phone from his pocket. He walked away from the table, answering his cell. As I sat there alone, I could see Miles through the windows of the restaurant pacing back and forth on the sidewalk. It seemed as if he was arguing. I certainly had no business exploring his mood, as I wasn't certain about my own. *Was I pissed, was I hurt? Was it a combination of both?* I didn't even know. I did know, however, that I loved Miles, even still.

Miles returned to the table, apologizing for the interruption. "Can we have a normal conversation now?" he asked as he sat back down in his seat. I wasn't ready, but I agreed to give it a go.

"Let's start over, Quinn. How've you been?" he asked again.

"Just velvety. I mean, I'm no surgeon, but I'm making it," I laughed at my own smartass remark.

He ignored my sarcasm and continued.

"A flower shop? You're a florist. Never pegged you as a florist," he stated.

"No, I'm not a florist. I work at a flower shop. And what did you peg me as? I'm curious," I asked.

"To be honest, traveling the world, playing music. You were gifted, Quinn. Do you still play?" he asked sincerely.

The truth was I never played again. After the night Brooks died, I never once picked up the violin. I wanted to scream that at the top of my lungs. Scream the horrible but accurate truth— *NO!! Actually, I became addicted to alcohol, Xanax, pain pills, cocaine, heroin, basically any form of drug, and I went to prison because you deserted me!!* But I didn't shout my reality. I was not ready for him to know who I had become. I was embarrassed and regretful, sadly acquainted feelings to me.

I answered, "Nope, not a musician." I took a sip of my water. *A glass of vodka would sure make this situation easier for me,* I thought. "How about you, Miles? Looks like you have succeeded. Doing what I always knew you would. Did you ever think about me? I mean after you left?" Wow. I couldn't believe I just came out with it so blatantly.

Just then the waitress came back to the table with our food in hand. I had ordered the lasagna and was boldly looking forward to it. I felt like Sam, salivating instantaneously at the lasagna's arrival.

The waitress situated our plates and refilled my water before leaving.

Miles had the most naturally perplexed look upon his face when I finally looked up at him. He sat back against his chair and crossed his arms across his chest before speaking. "Is that a serious question, Quinn?"

I felt paralyzed, unable to form any words. I was serious, but clearly, he was disgusted by my question.

"What the hell kind of question is that? Of course I thought about you. Every damn day, every minute. Why would you believe otherwise? I had to go, Quinn. I had no choice. But it didn't change the way I felt about you. It still hasn't." He had one single tear roll down his cheek. He quickly wiped it away with his napkin, and as I started to reach across the table for his hand, we were abruptly interrupted.

"Dr. Barlow, hello, how are you?" a woman asked as she loomed above our table. Miles was caught off guard as he attempted to snap out of our intense conversation and into professional form. He reached out his hand and said hello to the woman, who was obnoxiously flirting with him right there in front of me. *I mean, I could be his wife, bitch.* She evidently did not take that into consideration. *The audacity.* I picked up my phone as they bantered back-and-forth, pretending to scroll. It was a watery effort to conceal the irritation I felt.

After the husband-stealer left, we sat in silence, finishing our meal with a thick, tense atmosphere hanging between us. Neither of us knew what to say next. Miles broke the awkwardness by suggesting we leave. Grateful for the chance to cool down and catch my breath, I welcomed the idea of stepping outside. After we exited the restaurant, I felt slightly irritated by the lack of progression of our evening. I had accomplished nothing. As we started down the sidewalk, Miles began to reminisce aloud. "Remember that night we took the quilt out under our tree and watched the stars? The night you had a nosebleed, and we buried the blanket because we were afraid Frances would freak out about the blood on it?" he chuckled softly. I started to reply, my anger dissipating as I recalled that evening.

Mid-sentence, he seized me around the waist, pressing his lips and body against mine with force, leaving me no room to exhale. I yielded, even relishing the kiss, which seemed to linger for an eternity. It was intense, almost rough, catching me off guard. This was not what I anticipated. Miles had always been the only man whose kisses I truly cherished. In my years of addiction, there were countless "kisses," usually followed by indecent proposals for drugs. This was different, a refreshing change I had yearned for, waiting patiently.

Chapter **Then**

B Y THE TIME I was 15, Brooks was visiting my room during the late hours regularly. I could usually determine at dinner if I should prepare myself for his visit. By preparation, I mean escape mentally. I would memorize new music notes and play them in my head while he damaged me. More times than not, it worked, and I felt nothing. He was usually clever about his timing. Miles would be at the library in a study group or tutoring elsewhere. Other times I believed he or Frances would drug Miles to keep him from causing a ruckus by defending my honor. On the nights of occurrence, Miles would fall into a deep sleep so abruptly, unable to hold his eyes open, always waking the next morning feeling excessively groggy. We had no proof, but we suspected it.

My mother's presence was pretty much nonexistent at that point. She spent most of her time away on trips that Brooks would arrange for her. Her social status had grown after the marriage, and she had wealthy friends that were able to accompany her. I was aware that she had also become an alcoholic. When she was home, she could and would knock out an entire bottle of wine at dinner without help. I was so furious at my mother that I didn't care. We barely even spoke.

I felt as if she didn't love me, and our conversations weren't conversations at all. It was always her criticizing me about my choice of clothing or how I fixed my hair. I was never good enough. Miles said she was jealous of me. The only person that truly loved me was Miles—and Anna, before she was banished from the house.

One night, we sat at the dinner table as we always did, and my mother had prepared a roast with carrots and vegetables alongside. Apparently, the carrots were undercooked, sending Brooks into a fury. He cursed and shouted at Mother, ultimately flinging his plate at her hitting her in the face with it. Mother dared not make any sudden movements; she only flinched, instinctively touching her face and reaching for a napkin to wipe away the blood dripping from her cheek. It was too late; blood had dribbled onto the linen tablecloth lining the table. Frances criticized mother about the mess she was making of the linen. It was then that Brooks stood from the table, grabbing mother by the crown of her head, and dragging her away by her hair down the hallway. Frances pretended this was normal and resumed dinner as if nothing had occurred. So did we. Brooks never returned to the table that night, and I did not see my mother for about 2 weeks after that incident.

When my mother was finally freed from her room, she was covered in bruises and her hair had been cut. The bruises had faded, but I could still see them. Her demeanor was fine. She acted as if she had not been absent, carrying on her normal daily doings beside Frances. It was not long after that she had a ticket to Rome for 2 weeks with Brooks's colleague's wife.

Before Stella left for Rome, I wandered into her room. She was packing her suitcase and paused as I entered. For the first time in a long time, she looked me in the eyes. It was the one and only time I had ever seen regret in her stare. She walked over to me and wrapped her arms around me, saying nothing.

She only held me tightly as she began to weep softly. I didn't know why she was crying, but I could feel my eyes following suit. The hug didn't last long. She pulled away and wiped her tears with her hands and continued packing.

"Mom, please don't go," I shamefully begged of her. Those types of conversations were nonexistent at this point, but something made me optimistic. The hug had meant so much, had given me hope.

My mother again stopped packing and turned to me, her expression pained. "Quinn, I have to go. I must do as I am told, and so must you," she said softly, her voice tinged with sorrow. She cupped my chin and cheeks in her hands, her touch gentle and warm. "I love you," she whispered as tears streamed down my face, confusion and sadness overwhelming me.

She wiped away my tears, but they continued to flow uncontrollably. I clung to her affection, yearning for more of the motherly love I felt in that moment. "Quinn, please forgive me," she pleaded, turning away to resume packing. I sat on the edge of her bed, watching as she filled her suitcase, longing for our brief moment of connection to last.

I could not go with her; she needed to follow orders, leaving me behind despite the love we shared in that moment.

That was the last time I saw my mother. I was a few months away from my sweet 16 and closer to freedom from that house.

Chapter **Now**

I BROKE AWAY FROM his lips and slapped him across the face. It was impulsive, all my festering anger pouring out in that moment. Instant regret washed over me, and I quickly apologized, feeling the sting in my hand from the force of the slap.

"I'm sorry. I shouldn't have hit you," I said, my cheeks burning with a mix of embarrassment and fury. "What the fuck, Miles! It's been almost 10 years, and you show up at my doorstep like nothing happened. And Kent? He needed you; I needed you!" Tears welled up as I shouted at him.

Miles stared at his shoes, streetlights casting beams across his face, highlighting the red handprint on his cheek where I'd struck him. A couple passing by stared in disbelief.

"Move on, people! Everything's fine," I yelled, waving them off, a childish gesture from the new me.

Miles remained silent, still gazing at the sidewalk. His phone buzzed in his pocket, ignored. When he finally looked up, he soothed his cheek with a gentle rub before returning his hands to his pockets.

"I should go," he finally said. I couldn't tell if he was angry or humiliated. He had no expression upon his face.

He reminded me of Brooks, standing there seemingly void. I was left remaining there below the streetlight with only more questions. He turned away from me and began to walk away. I didn't stop him.

As I walked in the other direction the few blocks home, I fumed, replaying the whole evening in my mind on repeat. He had literally answered zero questions. I really craved a drink, just one. That would work, one drink, and that would suffice, I convinced myself. The Lucky Clover pub was near my house. I rounded the block and spotted it across the street. I could hear the music blaring as a group of girls my age were entering. I crossed the street and as I reached for the handle to enter, my phone rang. It was Sherry. I held the phone and watched it ring until it finally went to voicemail. *What a flipping reality check*, I thought. *Was this a sign?* I almost caved. I persuaded myself that I could have just one drink. *I am a fool.* By the grace of God, Sherry called me at the perfect time. Wow, maybe there is a god, and this was divine intervention. I returned Sherry's call on my walk home. Sherry didn't have much to say. She was informing me that we had two new participants joining us Thursday. She chattered about her cat and what she had made for dinner. She did that sometimes, reached out for no good reason. The timing, though, had never been better.

Sam was waiting happily at the door as I arrived home. wagging his tail and waiting for me to grab the leash to take him back down, and I did as I continued to listen to Sherry babble.

Kent was on my mind that night as I snuggled Sam close to me. I knew I needed to call him. I had done the same thing to him that Miles had done to me. Lying there in bed, thoughts of Kent flooded my mind. I remembered the aftermath of Brooks's disappearance and Miles's sudden departure. We were placed under the care of Brooks' cousin, Elena, the childless daughter of his uncle who had inherited a substantial fortune from her grandparents. Elena, though older and quiet, was kind, unlike Brooks. She took us into her home and focused on comforting Kent, who missed his father deeply.

While I was relieved Brooks was gone, Kent's longing for his dad made me resentful. I wasn't kind to Elena; in fact, I rarely spoke to her. With Miles absent, I was overwhelmed with grief and anger, which I directed at Elena by disregarding her rules. I stayed out late, mirroring the behavior of those who had hurt me, deliberately disobeying her.

Despite my hostility, Elena was a lifeline for Kent, rescuing and nurturing him during his time of need. *At least he had her,* I convinced myself before falling to sleep that evening.

But it was time. I would call Kent tomorrow.

Chapter Then

THREE WEEKS AFTER my mother left for Rome, I finally gained the courage to ask Frances when my mother would return. My mother was not answering or returning any of my calls. Our last conversation left me optimistic. Normally, I would never call or reach out, but I was holding on to possibility, positive that she would come back and things would change. It was then that Frances sat me down to tell me that my mother had killed herself. She was not sympathetic nor warm, and told me to keep this to myself as she would not allow my mother to tarnish the Barlow name. She added that my mother was a disgrace and that this was for the best. The story was mother died in a car crash in Rome, and that was that. I felt my eyes swelling up with tears, and as they did, she patted my knee and told me that my mother was a drunk and I was better off without her. She then stood, straightened her pant legs, and walked out of the room.

After she left, I fell to the ground and wrapped myself in the fetal position and sobbed uncontrollably. Miles soon came in and sat down beside me and gently ran his hands through my hair while I cried. He had clearly overheard Frances's cold explanation of what had happened to my mother.

"I'm sorry, Quinney," he whispered, pulling me up from the floor and dabbing my cheeks with a tissue. "Let's take a walk." My mother was never my ally, it seemed, but I loved her anyways.

"I'll grab a blanket and meet you at our tree," Miles said, disappearing upstairs. I agreed and made my way out to the spot.

I walked to the sycamore tree beside the creek and waited for Miles. We laid underneath it for what felt like hours. The sound of the creek flowing and the birds chirping brought me comfort. I could see the clouds peeking between the branches, and the leaves wrestling the winds, reminding me I could weather anything just like it had for so many years and still stand strong. It was peaceful and had always been my safe place. It was that day that Miles kissed me for the first time. Neither one of us knew what we were doing. He was so polite, asking me if he could kiss me before leaning in. Our foreheads bumped, and both of us giggled quietly before our lips finally touched. The kiss was simple, yet if I were standing, I believe my knees would have given out. He told me he loved me and that I was his best friend. He assured me that his grandmother would never hurt me again. Relief washed over me, knowing there was someone left on this earth that did love me. I leaned against his shoulder with my back against the tree and slept, dreaming of my dad and my mother too.

We were both brusquely awakened to Kent screaming. He was shouting out our names frantically. Miles jumped up and began running toward the house. The trail was about 100 yards long from the house to my tree, and the surrounding trees hid the path that we had made down to the creek. I tailed Miles to the house, unable to keep up. When I got there, I found the boys in the kitchen standing over Frances. She was lying on the floor motionless. She wasn't breathing and her lips were blue. Kent began shrieking, "Is she dead?" over and over. Miles turned and looked at me, expecting me to answer Kent.

"Kent, I don't know, have you called 911?" I asked him. Both Miles and I knew she was dead. He shook his head no, so I grabbed the phone sitting on the kitchen counter and dialed 911. Kent was kneeling beside Frances, shaking her aggressively and asking her to wake up. Kent was 13 but unable to process that she was gone. I assumed he was in shock after finding her this way. Miles sat calmly in the chair at the table gazing down at Frances's body on the floor, awaiting the arrival of help.

"No, she isn't bleeding, we don't know, we found her this way," I continued to tell the dispatcher. "Please, just send an ambulance," I demanded as I hung up on her.

Kent was now crying and shouting, "CALL DAD, CALL DAD!"

Miles and I just exchanged another glance, neither of us picking up the phone to call him. I was too scared. This would have to come from Kent. He would take it better from him. We both knew better.

I sat down in the chair next to Miles and waited for the ambulance. Miles grabbed my hand and squeezed it. He leaned in and whispered into my ear, "Everything is better this way." He then rose from his chair and made his way to Kent.

I sat there, a little taken aback from the lack of sadness and grief from Miles, and for a splint second, I wondered if he had done something to his grandmother. But my heart convinced me fairly quickly that he wasn't capable. He was now coddling Kent, kneeling beside Frances and attempting to pull Kent away from her. The paramedics had finally arrived, letting themselves into the house. They began to push Kent and Miles away from her while placing what looked like a device across her chest. A female paramedic gathered us three and escorted us to another room. Kent was still hysterical, almost gasping. He was asking the paramedic for his dad. She grabbed the cordless phone and dialed the number Kent was giving to her.

After a brief conversation, the lady hung up the phone. She looked directly at Miles and me. "Your dad is on his way. I'm sorry you kids had to find your grandmother this way. Stay in here, I need to go back in there to help," she said as she patted Kent on the shoulder as she left the room.

They were gone moments later, whisking Frances away on a gurney and out the door. Not long after that, Brooks arrived home smashing through the front door, hollering for Kent, never acknowledging me and Miles. And just as quickly as he stormed in, they stormed out. Miles and I assumed they were going to the hospital.

I sat there on the couch across from Miles feeling baffled about the events that had just transpired. Miles appeared calm and collected, like he wasn't surprised or rattled at all. I was still shaken and hurting about my mother, and now this. It was all so much to process, and my head felt heavy and my body felt beat. The truth was I wasn't sad about Frances, only shocked.

"Come on, Quinn, let's get out of here," he said as he stood up from the couch, appearing slightly eager. "Grab a bag and pack for a few days."

"What? I mean, where are we going?" I asked.

"Anywhere but here," he replied.

"But what about Kent?"

"What about Kent?" he said.

"We can't leave him here, Miles," I declared.

"And why not? He'll be fine."

"It's not right, and why're you so calm? Your grandmother just died; my mother's gone. I'm not good, Miles. I don't have the strength to leave right now." Anxiety surged, and I felt the urge to vomit.

Miles walked over close to me and tenderly pushed my

hair from my shoulder, then lightly brushed my face with his fingers. "I don't know. I just can't stand it anymore, Quinn. I've had enough."

"I need to go puke," I said as I jolted towards the bathroom holding my stomach. I caught a glance of myself in the mirror when I was done vomiting. I was colorless, and my eyes were sunken in. I looked awful. When I opened the door to come back out, Miles was standing there in the doorway.

"You're right, we can't just leave him," he said as he embraced me.

Chapter Now

I WOKE UP TO the sunlight peeking through my blinds. I grabbed my phone. 7:48. Surprisingly, Sam was still sleeping on the end of my bed. I sat up and scratched his head, waking him. His eyes were so innocent. He was a good dog, unconditional love. *Pretty pathetic that you're my only love, Sam,* I thought as I chuckled and began to dress. "Come on, let's go outside." I had a big day ahead of me. I had decided to drive to Beaufort to see Kent instead of calling him. I owed it to him.

On the drive over, I began to think about Anna. It had been so many years since she left, but I still often thought of her. She had clearly moved away and moved on, never giving me the opportunity to tell her what was really happening to me. Maybe if I had, she would have saved me. I was so embarrassed and scared that I never opened up to her. She had crossed my mind often in prison, not sure she even knew that I had gone away, if she did, she never wrote or called. I kind of hoped she didn't, so she couldn't be disappointed. I never had one visitor in prison, and I contemplated many times about ending everything. *Who would even miss me?*

The drive from Savannah to Beaufort wasn't far, but it was

worlds away for me. Savannah was a town filled with strangers, and I felt safer there than I ever had in Beaufort. Things sure would have been different for me if my dad had not died. He was like Sam. He loved me unconditionally. My dad talked a lot about Savannah. He loved that city. That was my main reason for settling down there after I was released.

I pulled up to the Beaufort police station, my hands shaking uncontrollably. Doubts flooded my mind, and I hesitated before even removing my hands from the steering wheel. What if he doesn't want to see me? What if he knows what happened to his dad? The uncertainty overwhelmed me. My skin felt like it was on fire, and sweat dripped down my forehead. This was worse than withdrawals. Taking a dramatic breath, I clutched the door handle, about to open it, when I saw the station door swing open.

There he was—Kent, walking alongside another officer toward a patrol vehicle. He looked the same, yet taller, his features more defined. Still handsome, but now with the look of a grown man. I watched him converse with the officer, finally waving goodbye. He paused, taking a call on his cell phone. I could see from a distance that it was a cheerful conversation; he smiled as he spoke. Maybe it wasn't about his dad that he had found out days ago. Just maybe.

Gathering my courage, I opened the car door and stepped out. Kent was still on the phone as I approached.

When he saw me, he paused. His face turned white, as if he had seen a ghost. "I'll have to call you back," he said as he hung up his phone. "My god—Quinn?" he said as he stepped back and bounced his head back in surprise.

I stepped closer and nodded at him. "Hi, Kent," I finally replied.

He stood there looking at me, as if it were a dream or a nightmare. I wasn't certain which. He didn't smile immediately, so I became flustered. "I wanted to see you, I guess. You're all grown up," I said as I meekly grinned at him.

He returned the smile and walked closer to hug me. It was an awkward hug, almost forced, but it was a nice act.

As the hug ended, more officers filed out of the station.

"You coming to lunch with us, Sheriff?" one asked.

"You guys go," he said, motioning for them to go ahead.

Turning back to me, he asked, "Lunch?"

"Sure, if you have time," I replied timidly.

"Okay, well, if you don't mind, just follow me. I need to take my own vehicle. I know a quiet place."

I agreed and returned to my car to follow him to lunch. *Okay, so that was uncomfortable,* I thought. Not really the warm welcome home I would have wished for, but understandably so. I had left him just like Miles had left me. What did I expect?

Chapter Then

THAT NIGHT IRONICALLY brought uncontrolled storms. The lights flickered on and off as we waited in anticipation for Kent and Brooks to return home. The rain pelted violently against the windows and the thunder attacked my ears, scaring me, causing me to jump each time. It sounded like a thousand horse hooves were coming for me. It reminded me of the wrath to come. Miles and I knew that Brooks would unload his emotions onto one of us. I imagined a roulette table, the little ball spinning around the table, waiting for it to land on one of us. I was denied the opportunity to even mourn the news of my mother's death. My mother, disconnected for so long, had looked at me differently the day she left for Rome. I saw a hint of love, regret, sorrow. *Did she apologize to me because her plan was killing herself all along and leaving me for the wolf?* It crossed my mind while I waited.

As the thunder still crashed, I thought I heard the doorbell ring amongst the noise. Miles had obviously heard the same ring, waking him from his sleep. It was a peculiar ring, elegant, seemingly matching the Barlow family who inhabited the home. Miles sprung from the couch, emerging a tad dazed from what was apparently a deep sleep.

"Was that the door?" he asked tensely, rubbing his eyes rather forcefully in attempts to wake himself further. He looked like a lost puppy, fearful and worried.

"Should we answer the door, Quinn? Who do you think it is? Look out and see if it's the police," he asked. This was rare; he was always so courageous and strong, even when wrestling with the beast Brooks. He was scared, and I wasn't sure of what. Why was he acting as if someone were about to show up and take him away? It was odd.

"Why would it be the police, Miles?" I said as the doorbell rang once more.

His shoulders were slouched, and his eyes were red and swollen, possibly from the aggressive rub he had given them seconds earlier. He was in rare form, almost paranoid. His clothes were wrinkled, and in this instant, they appeared to swallow his body. He looked like a small child. His plan was for us to escape, run away, and flee. But I had talked him out of it. I would not leave Kent to the wolf as my mother did me.

"Answer it, Miles." I gently nudged him towards the door, "You're acting strange."

I waited in the sitting room for him to return. I overheard the neighbor Mrs. Levine asking if there was anything she could do for us. He politely sent her on her way, assuring her we were okay. I assume she had seen the ambulance racing earlier and by now word had spread of Mrs. Barlow's passing. Her house was more than 200 yards away. Too bad she had never attempted to rescue us when we needed her. *Again, ironic,* I thought.

As Miles returned, he began pacing the room. "Quinn, we have to protect ourselves tonight. I know what's coming and so do you. What if he knows, what if they know what I have done?" He was now nervously folding his arms to his chest and unfolding briskly, over and over.

"What do you mean, Miles, what have you done? This isn't your fault, it's not mine either!" I exclaimed. My voice was high-pitched and cracked when I spoke. He was making the situation worse by panicking. I was standing next to him, following him while he paced. I placed my hand on his shoulder trying to comfort him as we marched around the room. When he finally stopped, he cupped his eyes to hide the tears. I felt uneasy, knowing there was nothing I could do. He was truly scared of what the evening would hold for us, and there was nothing I could do. The fury of Brooks's temper was indisputable.

Miles left the room, disappearing upstairs to his bedroom. I stood there frozen, unsure of my next move. I could hear him grappling around upstairs, and it sounded like he was launching things across his room. When he returned, he was holding a crowbar.

"What are you doing with that, Miles?" I asked hesitantly.

"I stole it from the back of his trunk a few weeks ago and hid it in my closet. For protection, Quinn."

Instantaneously, I began sobbing. "Miles, please, put it away," I pleaded. Before I knew it, I was clenching the crowbar, struggling to pull it from his grip.

After a brief struggle, he surrendered the crowbar and slumped to the floor. Holding it in panic, I feared what Brooks might do if he found us with it.

"Miles, I'm hiding this!" I shouted, dreading Brooks using it in a fit of rage.

Instinctively, I headed towards the basement. Off-limits and normally locked, it was dark and cold. Brooks had warned us about his storing dangerous pesticides and solvents down there. The flickering light switch revealed a room filled with old paint cans, light fixtures, and plastic bins. Blue barrels lined the walls.

As I reached for a bin to stash the crowbar, someone tapped my shoulder. I spun around in fear.

"Jesus, Miles, you scared the shit out of me!" I exclaimed, catching my breath.

"We shouldn't be down here. They could be home any minute," he declared loudly, urging me to go back upstairs.

"Just let me put this bar in here," I cried, maneuvering the plastic bin down from the shelf.

"Hurry up then," he said anxiously, fretting incessantly.

Opening the bin, I let out a horrifying squeal.

Chapter Now

I FOLLOWED KENT TO a small café about 15 minutes from the station. On the way over I felt my body tense up. I was thinking about all the mistakes I had made, fleeing to a new life, leaving Kent with basically a stranger. And immediately after losing his grandma and father all at once, I never even said goodbye to him, I just stopped visiting. *Was I there to apologize or seek answers about the body?* I didn't even know the answer to that myself.

I did learn how to interpret people when I was locked up. It was survival mode, and I was decent at it. My friend Helen taught me. It kicked in, and I could feel my adrenaline rushing and I felt a burst of self-assurance as I exited my vehicle to greet Kent at the door. *You have been through worse, Quinn*, I told myself as I flashed Kent a warm smile while he held the door open for me.

We entered the diner. It was pleasant, little red chairs surrounding each table and round bar stools perched on a silver shaft lining the round bar. The booths were lined with black-and-white checkered back splash, giving it a 60s vibe.

"Cute place," I said, reading the sign stating SEAT YOURSELF. "Booth or table?" I asked, turning to look at Kent.

"Booth," he said, leading the way. Setting my purse down, I followed and scooted in. As he sat across from me, he removed his cap and ran his hands through his dark brown hair. He must have resembled his mother, though I never saw a picture of her. There was no trace of her left when Stella and I moved in. His face was baby-like, with round cheeks and a small dimple below his chin, now more prominent than it was 10 years ago. His dark green eyes, which I had always found sweet, gazed back at me.

"Well, Quinn, this is a surprise. How are you?" Kent asked, jumping right into the conversation.

"I hope it's okay that I just showed up," I replied, sitting up tall and unraveling my napkin. My fork and knife clattered onto the table; I wanted him to know I wanted to be there.

"Certainly, it's definitely unexpected after all these years," he said, pushing the menu away. He seemed to know what he wanted; he'd been here before.

The waitress, an older lady in a white outfit with a red apron, approached the table. "Sheriff Barlow, nice to see you, sir. What can I get you? A coffee, black?" Her voice was raspy, as if she had just smoked a whole pack of Marlboro reds.

"That will work, Marla. Thank you," Kent replied.

"And for the lady?" Marla asked, still looking at Kent. He lowered his eyes and glanced over at me.

"I'll take an unsweet tea, please," I replied. The waitress never looked at me, only nodded at Kent and off she went.

Kent's eyebrows pulled closer together and the corners of his mouth drew downward, "What happened to you, Quinn?" he asked softly and genuinely.

I had never been asked that question. Only in group had I discussed in detail my downward spiral with drugs and alcohol. Kent knew I had been in prison by the look on his face.

"You know what happened to me, Kent," I said as I took a

deep breath and fiddled with my fork. I made direct eye contact as I replied.

I could see the sadness in his eyes after I replied. He wasn't to blame, and I know he loved me, back then anyway.

He looked down at the table with regret. "I don't know what to say, Quinn."

"Nothing you can say. I blame myself for my choices," I said as I felt one tear roll down my cheek. I swiftly wiped it away. "The drugs and alcohol, well, I coped the only way I could. But I am sorry, I mean, for running."

"I looked for you, saw you ended up in Edgefield Correctional. I almost came to see you. Wasn't sure what I would say to you," he said as he tilted his head to one side, still gazing downwards. "Elena, she was nice to me. She's a good woman. She's still around." He perked up slightly when speaking of Elena.

"You're married? I see you're wearing a ring," I said as we finally regained eye contact.

His demeanor changed; he sat up higher in the chair, displaying a proud grin across his face. "I have a baby on the way."

"I'm proud of you. And sheriff, too, that's great, Kent. Who is the lucky lady??" I asked sincerely.

"Nora Bates—well, Barlow now," he laughed proudly.

Nora Bates, Nora Bates, that name. I knew exactly what happened to Nora Bates.

"That is just great. You look genuinely happy; congratulations!" I said uncertainly as he began to stare down at his coffee, appearing lost in thought. "She had a sister my age that disappeared, Sara Bates?"

"Yes, that's her. Terrible thing. That family has been through the ringer," he responded, sniffling a tad before continuing, "We found her body this week near Albergotti Creek," he finished, seeming visibly upset.

Chapter **Then**

"W HAT!" MILES SHOUTED at me, "What is it Quinn, what's in there?" he said as he yanked the box towards him to look for himself.

I was stooping over the bin with my hand over my mouth, horrified at my findings.

"What are these?" he asked disbelievingly as he picked up the polaroids by the handful, some tumbling back into the bin.

"Oh god, what are these?"

"Just put them back, Miles. We can't get caught down here," I said as I snatched the pictures out of his hand and tossed them back into the box. I thought my eyes were betraying me. There were dozens of photos of teenage girls and boys half naked tied with rope of some sort. They looked dirty and beaten. I was sick, again, and before I could find a trash can, I spewed vomit onto the floor.

"Shit, Quinn!" Miles whispered in an obvious frenzy. We could hear footsteps upstairs. Brooks and Kent had made it home. I shoved the bin back onto the shelf and left the vomit on the floor. We tiptoed up the stairs of the basement and shut it quietly.

Kent was standing in the kitchen, his clothing drenched with rainwater as Miles and I emerged from the basement. He had been crying, still wearing red-stained cheeks and puffy eyelids. He was holding a glass of milk and paused as he saw us. "Where's Brooks?" I whispered to him quietly. Miles was now hugging Kent while remaining silent. He welcomed Kent's head into his chest and wrapped him up in his arms.

Kent kept quiet and only shrugged his shoulders in response to my question while continuing to drink the milk from his glass. I decided it was best to sneak off to my room and shut the door. I pushed my dresser over in front of the door just in case Brooks came looking for me later. The house was noiseless and gloomy, the rain still attacking the windows. As I settled onto my bed, I coiled my knees up to my chest and prayed.

What felt like an eternity had passed. I heard the pitter-patter of steps coming closer to my door. Miles muttered softly through my door, "Kent is staying with me tonight." I said nothing back. I was sad for Kent; he loved his grandmother, and I'm sure he was heartbroken, but my adrenaline was still flowing, and truthfully, I was glad she was gone.

I lay there, and all I could think about was the plastic bin. It had me disturbingly alarmed. What was that? Old pictures from trials? Crime scene photos? He was, after all, a judge. What kind of sick or disturbed person keeps those things in their home? I didn't understand it. Brooks was a monster; I already knew that, but this was another level of revulsion.

Between the photos, Miles's strange behavior, Frances, and my mother's death, I was drained. I had nothing left; I was overwhelmed to the max. I continued to pray that night for safety from Brooks, not just for myself but for the boys too. I prayed for my mother and my dad, and I prayed for a way out. I had never prayed more.

As a family, we attended church—well, minus my mother most of the time; it was for show. Brooks was no godly man.

He was an imposter, a fake. He paraded us around the pews like we were one big happy family, smiling and greeting the church members. Just like everything else, it was a mirage, smoke and mirrors for the people. But in that moment, I was thankful I had learned how to ask God for help, and I did just that.

Chapter **Now**

His mood had totally changed. Kent was no longer sitting tall; he was slouching once again. He continued, "I shouldn't be talking to you about this."

The waitress returned, asking if we were ready to order while refilling our beverages.

"Quinn," he said as he looked over at me waiting for me to order and trying to gather himself for the waitress.

"I'll take the club sandwich please, with mayonnaise and French fries," I said as I handed her the menu.

"I'll have the same, Marla, thank you."

"I'll have that right out," she said with a head nod as she grabbed his menu and shuffled towards the kitchen.

I remembered back then hearing at school more than once about a slew of missing girls. The kids at school would ask me questions about it, like I should have answers because Brooks was a judge.

"Nora told me she didn't run away. She knew something awful had happened to her sister, and she was right," Kent persisted as he balled up his fists in anger.

"Kent, I remember more than Sara going missing. Our town

was full of young girls labeled runaways. It was peculiar. Maybe none of them ran away," I presented.

"Don't get too far ahead of yourself, Quinn. We have no idea what happened to Sara. The coroner was uncertain about cause of death. It could have been a terrible accident. I intend on finding out. I don't know why we are even talking about this." He started to pause. "Why are you here?" he added suddenly.

Just then his phone rang, disrupting the tense silence between us. As he reached for it, I paused, internally debating my next move.

Our food had not even come, and Kent placed his cap back on his head as he listened intently to someone on the other end. He began sliding out of the booth slowly. He covered the phone with his hand as if to mute himself. "I have to go, Quinn," he then took out a card from his shirt pocket as he stood and set it on the table. "Call me soon," he said as he pressed the phone back to his ear and exited the diner in a hurry.

I sat there alone in the booth as Marla approached. "Duty called, little lady?" she inquired as she grabbed his coffee cup and hovered above me waiting for me to answer.

"Looks like it, Marla. I'll take my club to go please."

Marla turned away and groaned. *Well, isn't she a gem,* I thought to myself.

During the drive home I felt restless. *Okay, it wasn't Brooks.* I was thankful for that, anyway. The last time I saw Brooks, he was lying on the basement floor bleeding from his head.

*   *   *

Sam greeted me at the door. "Hey there, Buddy, you miss me?" I said as I touched his head playfully and grabbed the leash to accompany him downstairs. "You are a pain in the ass, Sam, you know that?" I said as we made our way down.

My phone rang as I sat watching Sam sniff every possible inch of the grass available to him. It was Sherry. *Shit.* I had completely forgotten about group this evening. I also missed two calls from Claudia. I'm certain she was inquiring when I was returning to work. I had not yet listened to her voicemails.

"Hi, Sherry."

"You okay? I missed you this evening," she expressed with concern in her voice. I rarely missed therapy, and Sherry was justified in sounding worried.

"I'm okay. I have been exhausted, that's all. You don't have to worry, it's nothing. Scout's honor," I said as I laughed sarcastically.

"Should I drive over?" she asked hesitantly.

"Sherry, seriously I'm fine. I assure you. I'm just truly exhausted. I hit my head pretty hard, cut me some slack."

"No pain pills, right?" she quizzed.

"NO pain pills," I answered confidently. "I'll be there next week; we can have dinner after group, okay?" I said.

I loved that Sherry kept me accountable. Even though I still found her pesky, I was grateful she cared.

Sherry said good night and Sam and I returned upstairs to settle in.

The truth was I did still think about numbing the anguish, but I fought it. I would meditate or scroll the internet, anything to keep my mind busy, or clear.

They found Sara's body. I wondered how many more would turn up. After all this time, Brooks may finally be exposed. But I was hoping not to be.

.

Chapter Then

THE NEXT MORNING, I awoke to my alarm. I had drifted
to sleep, and surprisingly, never woke. My body had
turned off, and I was relieved for the rest after such
a night. As I moved the dresser from the door, I felt a sense
of relief. Brooks had not bothered me throughout the night,
and I decided I had no choice but to tackle what the day held
for me, although I still feared Brooks's temper. I wanted to
ask Brooks more about my mother, but clearly, I would not.
It wasn't the time. He would be in an upset state about his
own mother, and I was asking for trouble if I mentioned my
mother. I decided against it, thinking maybe I would gain the
courage at a later time. *Would we honor Frances's life and not
my mother's? Would he have a service for both? Did anyone
even know my mother had passed? How did she do it? Who was
she with in Rome?* I had so many unanswered questions that
would unfortunately have to wait.

I made my bed as I was supposed to. I could hear the boys
emerging from their rooms and making their way down the hall.
I was thankful we had school that day, praying Brooks would
allow us to go. I got ready quickly just in case he permitted it. It
was a protected place, no Brooks to avoid.

I had made a few friends, although I never saw them outside of school. I didn't fit in; they wore all black, and most of them looked like they hadn't washed their hair in months. I didn't care; they were accepting, nonjudgmental. I felt defiant when I was with them, almost a silent fuck you to Brooks, knowing he would not approve.

Miles was a loner. He spent most of his time with his head in the books. He always spoke to me in passing, however. Our last names were different, but everyone knew I was part of the Barlow clan, and it probably kept me from being bullied, Miles as well. No one messed with a Barlow, not even the teachers.

Kent was still in middle school, and I assumed with his last name he was also fine. He was into sports, playing on the junior high football team as quarterback. I looked forward to his games; I felt normal if only for a few hours. We were always expected to sit as a family, but even so, the outings were a reprieve. Sometimes Stella would join; sometimes she wasn't able. She would either be hiding bruises, or she was drunk or out of town.

I managed to dodge Brooks that morning. I never heard him come out of his room. I made the boys breakfast, assuming we were to do what we always did, unless otherwise instructed. Miles was old enough to drive, but yet to get a car. I could only imagine why.

It was March, a few weeks away from my 16th birthday and a few months away from Miles graduating from high school. I continued to play back the night before in my head throughout the day. *Would Miles actually leave Kent and I with Brooks when he graduates? Would he wait on us? He wanted to leave last night; I reasoned him out of it.* I was concerned about Kent. Without us there, would Kent become Brooks's target? I didn't want that for him.

"Hey, Quinn," I heard Nathan shout across the hallway.

He was approaching me. He was the leader of the goth pack at school, and we were somewhat friends, more of acquaintances really. He always paid special attention to me at school, and I didn't mind it. Nathan had attempted to appear more "emo" by dying his blonde hair black, but his blonde roots peeked through at the crown. His nails were always painted black, and he wore a chain that fell from his pocket. "We're ditching 5th period and meeting under the bleachers, wanna come?" he asked. I knew I shouldn't, but strangely I agreed. "Yeah, sure," I said nonchalantly as I shrugged my shoulders, like I wasn't terrified of getting caught. It felt invigorating to make a decision on my own, particularly one Brooks wouldn't be proud of.

Under those bleachers during 5th period changed everything. For once, I felt in control of my own being. It was the first time I got high, and the high made me forget. I forgot about Brooks, I forgot about my mother, I forgot about my pain, and I forgot about the pictures I had seen. I was fascinated by this feeling, I craved more of the sensation instantly, the intoxication pulling me into utopia. The drug was a remedy to a kinder world. My existence welcomed me, even nurtured me. I felt alive. Relaxing was an understatement; the tension exited my body and I felt like I was 5 years old again, without a worry in the universe. Brooks had shaken my innocence somewhere along the way, but that day, that experience transformed me.

I did not return to school that day, nor did I return home immediately after school.

Chapter Now

I DECIDED TO RETURN to work the next morning, calling Claudia on the way. She was pleased that I was coming. Apparently her husband had severe arthritis, and the tedious work was difficult for him.

I was in the back putting on my apron and looking over orders when Claudia appeared. "You had a visitor yesterday," she proclaimed.

"A visitor? Who was it?" I asked curiously.

"She wouldn't leave her name. A lady, older than you, very pretty. She said she would drop in another time," she said as she shrugged her shoulders and continued to grab some tulips to take to the front.

I speculated who it could have been. I have zero friends except Sherry, and to be honest, no one would describe her as pretty.

I walked up front. "What did she say?" I asked Claudia. She was putting together a beautiful arrangement of yellow tulips.

"You know, not too much, she seemed to be in a hurry. She was only in here for a few minutes. Oh, she left you something though. Let me grab it." She put down her bouquet of yellow tulips and proceeded to the register reaching under the shelf below. She pulled out something from the shelf and walked back over, handing me a small box wrapped in tissue paper.

I told her thank you and proceeded to the back. As I examined the box, I wondered, *Who on earth would have brought me a gift?* I looked at it for several minutes like I had been handed a magic bean or something.

I began to unwrap the tissue . . . It was a box of chocolates. Dark chocolate truffles, the same kind Anna used to sneak into the house for me years ago. *Anna?* I thought. Stumped, I was trying to process the idea that Anna had come to visit me. *How would she know where to find me? And why, after all this time?* We had lost contact after I went to prison.

It can't be. It must be a mistake. Surely this was a blunder on Claudia's part. Maybe it was meant for delivery, an addition to a flower arrangement. There was no card, no message. Claudia must have misconstrued this. She had, after all, mixed up orders before. *Yeah, that explains it.*

I did not think about the chocolates for the remainder of the workday. Claudia was right; we were busier than normal, and the time flew by. By evening, Sam was thrilled to see me. I warmed myself up a can of soup and flipped on the television. The first day back, all day on my feet made me extra tired.

To my surprise, Sara Bates's name was splashed across the screen: Breaking News; Authorities have identified human remains as those of Sara Bates, an 11-year-old female gone missing 14 years ago from Beaufort, SC. Police have now discovered more bodies buried along the creek bank of Albergotti Creek.

I clutched my chest. My heart raced a million miles an hour. I knew it!!!! Those plastic bins were filled with those missing girls' pictures. I knew what this meant. I knew Brooks hurt those girls; he had done more than hurt them, he had murdered them. He was revolting. He kept those pictures as trophies.

Such a callous disregard for human life. I sat there in a dazed manner. Should I pick up the phone and call someone? Who would I call? Kent? *Hello, Kent, your dad murdered all those girls.* No one would believe me; I was the troubled teen with prison time to prove it. I desperately needed to see Miles.

Chapter **Then**

I SPENT THE REST of the day and the evening in an abandoned house on the outskirts of town, declining all of Miles's persistent calls on my cell. Nathan had started a fire, and it was surrounded by about 10 kids from school, some I didn't even know, all labeled misfits or outcasts; and then there was me, the rich kid acting out. Nathan handed me my first drink, vodka with cranberry. I didn't like it, but I swallowed it anyways. The feeling I had after one was remarkable. I felt like a survivor, with a woozy disposition. I knew I would have to go home, but for now, I was very okay. I was indulging in everything I knew Brooks would disapprove of, and it felt energizing.

Tonight was the beginning of a new beginning. I would face Brooks with a fearless face, a new me when I returned home. Nathan called it liquid courage, and it was. I threw my backpack on my shoulder and hitched a ride back into town. It was 11:30 when I pulled into the driveway. I could still smell the faint scent of marijuana on my clothes and the vodka on my breath. The house was dark, except for the security lights detecting me as I approached the door. I turned the knob to find it unlocked. I entered, gently shutting the door behind me. To no surprise, the light abruptly flickered on.

Brooks was standing there in the entryway glaring at me with wicked eyes, seething with obvious rage. "Your grandmother passes away, and this is how you pay respects to her?" he said as he smoldered with fury.

"She was NOT my grandmother," I hastily replied. The liquid courage I was warned of earlier in the evening spewed out.

His temper sparked, he lunged towards me, and his open hand immediately met my face. My face instantly throbbed as I witnessed raw anger visibly flow through him. I was still woozy, losing my balance and falling to the ground. His fists were balled, and my body began to tremble, anticipating the next blow. He towered above me, waiting for me to beg, to plead for him to stop. I wouldn't, not tonight.

"GO TO HELL, BROOKS!" I courageously shouted at him as I kicked up at him from the tile.

By this time, Miles was standing on the top of the stairs, watching in disbelief. Brooks grabbed my hair and began pulling me towards the kitchen across the hard, cold tile. I never once asked him to stop, which only infuriated him more. I concluded he got satisfaction from his abuse of power and strength. He got pleasure in knowing he scared me. I did, however, fight back. I felt faint, but with little strength I did have I clawed at him, unable to deter him or lighten his death grip from my hair. I could hear Miles racing down the stairs as my legs continued to slide across the tile. When we reached the kitchen he opened the cabinet, all the while never releasing me from his grasp. He threw me back to the ground and hurled his body on top of mine. I felt his hand clinch my neck, the other holding an open bottle of whiskey. I braced myself for the torture, I only prayed quietly that Miles would save me. Miles dashed to my side, his hand outstretched toward Brooks's shoulder in a desperate attempt to intervene.

In a swift and brutal move, Brooks's elbow slammed into Miles's ribs, sending him careening into the corner of the cabinet with a forceful crash.

Unrestrained, he screamed, sounding as if he were possessed, "Is this what you want? I'll give you what you want!" He forced open my jaw and began pouring the whiskey into my mouth. Small raspy gasps escaped my mouth. The whiskey burnt my throat as his fingers dug harder into my jaw.

I could hear Miles faintly in the background. He was yelling at Kent to get back upstairs. I opened my eyes as Brooks ran out of whiskey to waterboard me with. I began to cough excessively, still trying to catch my breath. A wave of calmness came across Brooks. He was still sitting on top of me but had released his hand from my face. He bent over closer, touching his nose to mine. Sweat dripped from his forehead, showering my face. I could hear his heart beating against his chest. "Next time you disrespect me, I will kill you and get away with it."

The hairs on the back of my neck stood up. He meant it, and I believed him.

Chapter **Now**

I JUMPED UP FROM the couch. I was going to march down to the hospital and hopefully catch Miles at work. I had no idea where he lived, and this was a conversation I wanted to have in person. He saw those pictures; he was there that night with me. He would know what to do.

I pulled up to the ER entrance. The parking lot was full and scattered with people smoking and families waiting. I saw an older man half naked appearing to escape in a wheelchair, hurriedly hobbling the chair further from the door. He had made it halfway across the parking lot when what I assumed was his son grabbed the wheelchair, whipping it back towards the ER.

The ER summoned memories I'd rather forget. Too many hours and days seeking fleeting relief within those walls. Stepping through the doors, I wondered if Miles was one of those doctors who catered to my requests, fueling my addiction. Or was he different—compassionate, offering options, asking questions, making referrals?

"Excuse me, ma'am, can I assist you?" A small woman with a cropped haircut repeated her question as I stood lost in thought, waiting my turn at the front desk.

"Oh, yes—I am here to see Miles Barlow. I mean, um, Dr. Barlow," I said hesitantly as the lady behind me exhaled loudly with irritation. I turned to look at her, she was standing there with her hands crossed at her chest. She rolled her eyes at me, and I turned back around to the lady at the desk.

"Ma'am, what is going on? Are you injured? I can get you seen, I just need to know what the issue is."

"Oh no, I mean, I don't have an issue, or an injury. Dr. Barlow is a friend. I need to see him."

"Yeah . . ." The lady paused. I could tell she was searching for a polite way to tell me to get lost.

"Look here, you need to either tell the lady what's up with you or get gone. You are holding up the line." I heard the lady's voice come from behind me. Her arms were now uncrossed, appearing even more impatient than before. Her hip was turned out and one hand had made its way to the hip. She was eyeballing me up and down intensely. Her brow was furrowed, and I could tell she was prepared for confrontation. *Nope, not today. I won't do it.* I politely stepped away and let her move in front of me, staying silent.

I sat down and dug out my cell phone from my purse. *I'm in ER waiting room. I need to talk to you.* I sent Miles a text.

As I waited patiently, I watched the lady that was so blatantly rude to me check in. I could spot a drug seeker from a mile away, and she fit the bill. However, I could tell she was new to it. *You never walk in and tell them what works. Amateur,* I thought.

As the lady passed me to sit back down and wait, I wanted to grab her, shake her, yell at her to go home. Instead, I combed through my purse again. I found a card, stood up, and approached her. Holding out the card, she hesitated before taking it, reading the words quietly. "Hopeful House."

"You're not alone," I whispered, turning away and returning to my seat. Surprisingly, Sherry would have been proud of me.

Before I even managed to sit back down, I saw Miles through double doors as they swung open. I stood there waiting for him to motion me over.

He did, waving me through the doors, and I obliged, following him to a small office with computer screens and monitors displaying heart rhythms and such. We sat before he spoke; he was wearing his white jacket again, but this time I noticed stubble surrounding his cheeks and jawline. I had not seen him with stubble, and it made him look older. I didn't mind it.

"It's busy today, Quinn. I don't have much time. You okay?" he finally spoke.

"Listen, I'm sorry about slapping you," I said, catching myself gnawing at my cuticle, a side effect of feeling uneasy.

"Don't apologize, really. I guess I deserved it," he said, rubbing his cheek softly as if it were still sore.

As I looked for evidence across his face that I had slapped him, it was absent. No slap marks to speak of.

"Have you seen the news?" I asked, about to mention more about the situation when a red-headed nurse, rather pretty, burst through the door. "We have an MVA on the way, critical passenger," she announced swiftly and then left as quickly as she appeared.

"I'll come by tonight. We can talk more," he said, rising from his rolling chair and exiting the room.

I made my way through the crowd gathered in the hallway of the ER, family waiting anxiously on what I assumed was the MVA. I knew what it meant through my many trips to the ER. Someone had had a motor vehicle accident, and the family was gathered to wait for their loved one's arrival.

It made me think of my dad, that fateful day we lost him. Mother and I stood in a hallway just like this one anticipating his arrival. I wasn't crying, though. I wasn't sure what was happening at that moment, but I do remember my mom shedding a few tears and telling me I would be alright and not to worry. I felt sympathy for the family and wanted so much to reach out and hug them, but instead, I kept walking, showing myself to the exit.

$\mathscr{Chapter}$ Then

ROOKS GOT UP off the top of me and wiped away the sweat from his forehead. He straightened up his shirt and made his way out of the kitchen as if nothing had happened. I remained frozen there on the floor with my hair and face still drenched in whiskey. Within seconds Miles was kneeling beside me lifting my head from the tile. I felt light-headed and sick to my stomach as he did, my head still swirling, still trying to catch my breath. "Quinn, you okay? I'm sorry," he murmured as he attempted to console me by pressing my soaked head into his chest. By this time Kent had appeared and he was sobbing, his face saturated with tears. I looked up at Kent, signaling at him that I was okay. This settled him down somewhat.

Miles helped me off the floor to the stool around the bar. I was wiping the whiskey from my face with my hands the best I could, my hair dripping wet, the stout smell of the liquor invading the room and my nose. I was still coughing as Kent handed me a rag to clean up with. Miles wasn't sure what to do, so he began taking rags and using them to soak up the remnants of liquor off the floor. We all knew this mess could not be there when Brooks woke the next morning.

I needed to lie down, specifically in my bathroom close to my commode. I had a feeling the alcohol would be making its way out quickly by the feeling of nausea overcoming my body. Kent and Miles helped me to my bathroom, and I puked for most of the night, clutching the side of my toilet like my life depended on it. Miles was there holding my hair back and wiping my mouth periodically, Kent sitting in the corner, seemingly scared to death. I hated that Kent had seen me this way. I felt a hint of remorse for my behavior causing such a vile scene.

Miles's presence meant the world to me that night. He didn't say much but he felt like my salvation that night, and I knew I would survive. However, Brooks threat to me replayed throughout my head like a song on repeat, causing my temples to feel like they were about to burst any minute, making the all the pain even worse. This only seemed to provoke the heaving and vomiting drastically. The look in his eyes, the tone of his voice, the way *I will kill you* rolled out of his mouth so naturally. If he kept that promise, I knew it wouldn't be his first time.

That night, the boys huddled close to me in my room. Miles enveloped me with one arm, Kent with the other. The weight of my despair pressed heavily against my chest, and in that darkened room, I pitied myself. With tears streaming down my face, I whispered into the quiet of the night, asking God why He didn't love me. Why had He taken both my parents from me? How could He abandon me to the care of such a devil?

Anger simmered within me, boiling over into a seething resolve. It was my breaking point, the moment where anguish turned into determination. As Miles and Kent held me close, I made a silent vow that echoed through the darkness: this was the last time I would speak to Him.

I woke up the next morning with a tumultuous headache. I had no choice but to get up and get ready. I knew that today was the day of Frances's funeral, and surprisingly, Miles had found out that morning that Brooks was also holding a memorial for my mother. I knew it was a show for the town, so it looked as if he was a loving widower who had just lost his wife and mother, but I didn't care. I wanted to celebrate that very last moment that me and my mother had shared, and I held on to that while I pushed through the morning. I would embrace the opportunity to revel in her memory, the glimpse of love she showed me that day. And in some sick way, I did love her. Or maybe it was more I wanted her to love me. I wasn't sure. I was a lost and confused almost 16-year-old girl.

The entire town gathered for the funeral. Brooks had woken up in a surprisingly pleasant mood. He acted as if he didn't waterboard me with whiskey and almost kill me the night before, so I just rolled with it. I had put on my best dress and helped Miles fix his tie before leaving the house. There was a stretch of cars for as far as I could see. I wondered how many people were actually here to pay respects to my mother. She had a convincing brave face when she fronted to the town, especially before her drinking evolved. People liked my mom. She was a lot like Brooks; she knew how to fake it. Stella had many faces, and sometimes I wondered if I was just like her.

I was hugged over and over all day, people telling me how sorry they were for my losses. While some crying as they squeezed me, I never shed a tear. I was on autopilot, just as I saw my mom so many times. I hated myself. I wanted to whisper in every ear what a beast Brooks was and to please rescue me, but I didn't. I hugged them back and gave a slight smile as they moved along. I couldn't help but think about what would happen to me now. I wasn't technically a Barlow, so maybe he would send me away. That was my hope. But would he? No. That wouldn't look respectable on his part. No, I was still a prisoner, I decided.

The line began to get shorter; it eased my mind some as my legs were tired and I still felt the soreness from the night before. I had no physical marks displayed, but I felt sore in my jaw and my chest. I was ready to go home and rest, or better yet, run off with my new friends and escape to my newfound bliss. As I gazed towards the end of the line, I saw Anna in the distance, looking directly at me with kindness—or was that guilt I sensed in her eyes? She was standing alone by an old tree, almost as if she were hiding from someone. I looked away for less than a minute, and when I turned back around, Anna was gone as quickly as she had appeared. I never had the chance to have even a small conversation with her, and it saddened me.

Miles and Kent had been preoccupied with the invasion of mourners and relatives; I was on my own. My mother did not have a casket, only a partition of photos and flowers with her name etched in gold across the top. It was nice and simple, unlike my mother. There was a headstone beside Frances's that read "Stella Barlow, loving wife and mother." I knew my mother would never agree to be buried, or rested, next to Frances. She despised her, she had to have. *But where was my mother's casket? Where was her body?*

Chapter **Now**

MILES ARRIVED AT my house at 8:46 p.m., with Sam welcoming him at the door with a tail wag and a friendly howl. He was still wearing his scruffy shadow on his jaw along with his scrubs. He appeared tired, like he had had a long day, his body drooping as if it were going to give out any moment.

I had prepared for his arrival, doing my best to appear somewhat put together. I had my best jeans on with a light blue tank top. He always loved blue; I wasn't sure why I didn't want to disappoint him.

"Come in, sit down. Can I get you anything? Something to eat, something to drink? You look tired," I said as I stood in the kitchen waiting for a response. He never sat down, only followed me to the kitchen.

"You have a beer? I'll take a beer" he replied.

"I actually don't. I have water," I replied as I shrugged my shoulders with slight humiliation.

"Whiskey?" he asked. *The audacity,* I thought.

I saw his eyes widen. "I'm sorry, I didn't . . ." He paused. "I'll take a glass of water, thanks."

I opened the cupboard and grabbed a glass and began filling

it with ice and water. My hands were shaky for some bizarre reason. I presumed his presence still made me nervous.

As I handed him the glass, we headed to the living room, and his body melted onto the couch. I sat across from him stiff as a board.

"Have you heard the news? There have been so many bodies found back home. Have you talked to Kent?" I asked anxiously, assuming he hadn't seen the news due to work.

He took a long swig of water before responding. "I haven't spoken to Kent yet. He left me a voicemail earlier today, but I was swamped in the ER and then rushed right over here."

"Call him back. Look, I recorded the news, Miles. You have to see this," I said, rising from the couch to search for the remote.

"Do you want me to call him back or do you want me to watch the news?" he asked snidely.

I rolled my eyes, not making eye contact, and persisted to turn on what I had previously recorded.

"Miles, this is serious. They found bodies, multiple. I know it was Brooks. He killed all those girls. We saw those pictures. Remember Sara Bates? They found her. Miles, I saw her photo in that bin, and so did you."

He sat up straighter on the couch, leaning forward towards the television. "Turn it on," he insisted. He interlocked his hands, and his cheeks had turned a dark shade of red. I could tell he was uneasy, focused on the TV, awaiting the misery to come.

We watched in utter disgust and neither one of us said a word. Four girls had been found around the creek, uncovered only after construction began for a boat ramp and structure. This would make five bodies all together, and we both knew there could be more. That bin was filled with more than five photos. I began to consider that maybe Brooks had not murdered them all, but I had no idea what to reason. The only one I recognized was Sara Bates. I had met her once before she "ran away."

I clicked off the TV and looked over at Miles. He was staring down at the floor as if time had stood still. He was motionless and dumbfounded.

He finally spoke with a fracture in his expression. "This is an impossible situation, Quinn. You understand that, right?"

"What do you mean? How so? We both know Brooks did this. What did you do with that bin full of photos, Miles?" I asked him as I felt myself becoming eager.

"I didn't do anything with that bin, Quinn," he said back rather hostilely. "What did you do with that bin?" he asked accusingly.

"It was gone when I went back down there. I assumed you moved it before the police started looking around for Brooks," I answered.

The conversation felt tense. I stood to pace the room and gather my thoughts.

"Stop pacing, Quinn. It's making me nervous. If you didn't take the bin and I didn't take the bin, where the hell is it?" he exclaimed. "And what are we supposed to do? Run up there and tell Kent, oh hey, your dad killed your wife's sister? Come on, Quinn, what good would that do?" he said. He walked to the kitchen with his glass in hand, Sam following him. He bent over to scratch Sam's head. "Have you also forgotten what we did?" he quietly asked as he continued to rub Sam's head, never looking up at me.

"Of course I haven't forgotten!" I screamed at him. I was still standing, now holding my stomach as I began to feel queasy. I had an urge for a drink, something to numb this agony. I continued to holler, "Forget? How could I forget? My fucking life is in shambles, Miles! I went to prison—I am an addict! But you? You seem to be just fine! Let's just sweep this under the rug because you have this amazing life to get back to! You made it, congratulations! You beat the odds; I wasn't so lucky!"

"Don't you dare blame me, Quinn," he shouted back. It was full-blown war, and I could see a distant look emerge upon his face. He was infuriated. He slammed the glass onto the counter, sending it sailing into pieces. Sam had disappeared to the bedroom as the yelling continued. "You'll wish you had just kept your mouth shut, Quinn! Goddamn you!!" he said as he headed for the door.

He reached for the knob and paused, then turned around to look at me. "What we did, huh?" His voice carried an edge of anger as he shook his head subtly. "You're crazy," he added before storming out of my apartment.

Chapter Then

AFTER THE FUNERAL, we made it home, accompanied by a plethora of people. The house was filled with family and friends of the Barlows, along with brownies, casseroles, and crock pots. We could have fed the entire town from our kitchen, it seemed. Brooks had remained silent on the drive home. We were accompanied in the limo by a fellow judge, an apparent friend of Brooks, along with his wife, which I was grateful for. It meant we didn't have to be alone with Brooks. His colleague's wife's name was Susan. She was one of my mother's friends. In fact, she was the one I believed that my mother had left for Rome with, but I wasn't certain.

Miles had been quiet during the happenings of the day, and I had noticed he never shed a tear. I wasn't sure he loved Frances. He would often talk about how vile she was to me and my mother, and I wondered if that was the reason. Had I unintentionally robbed him of loving his own grandmother? A gush of guilt pierced my soul. I hoped not, but after all, she was vicious.

I was able to sneak out and head to my safe place, under my tree. I sat below the tree and listened to the birds chirp and the breeze bustle throughout the leaves. It was midday, and the

sun was still shining, peeking in and out of the limbs, hitting
my face just right. My head rested against the sturdy trunk,
reminding me that it was alive and well. It was always there,
waiting for me to come and unload the days' occurrences. I had
left Miles tending to Kent. He had been sobbing hysterically at
the funeral and was still weeping on the drive home. He needed
Miles today, and I understood that.

As I closed my eyes in an attempt to flee from reality,
I could hear leaves crunching, warning me that someone was
approaching. It was Susan. "You okay, sweetheart?" she asked
gently as she kneeled down close to me.

Susan and I had never had an actual conversation. It was
usually an exchange of an insincere hello or goodbye, so I was
initially caught off guard by her presence.

By that time, she had sat crisscross right beside me in the
leaves, and I instinctively moved over a bit as I felt a little
crowded by her company.

"I'm okay," I uttered, still unsure why she was there.

She placed one hand upon my knee and looked up at the
sycamore tree. "This is a beautiful tree, peaceful to look at,"
she said as she gazed up at the branches. "I'm sorry; I watched
you walk out here, and I wanted to check on you is all," she
admitted.

"Thank you," I responded, feeling somewhat invaded by her
closeness even after scooting over. I knew this was the perfect
opportunity to prod about my mother. I opted to engage and
play the victim for some answers. I hung my head down low.
"Did you know my mother well?" I asked shyly.

She had removed her hand from my knee when I scooted
over, but she was still observing the surroundings. It was a
lovely spot, and if you listened carefully, you could hear the
creek rolling, the water filtering down the stream.

"I think I knew her fairly well. What she wanted me to know, anyways." She briefly hesitated. "I am sorry about your mother, Quinn. She talked about you a lot, you know."

"She did?" I questioned, surprised by her admission.

"Yes, she did. She was proud of you. She said you were so gifted, incredibly intelligent, and very tough. She was very proud," she returned. She was now looking me in my eyes.

I broke the awkward eye contact and began to rustle the leaves occupying the space around me. "Were you there? With her in Rome?" I finally asked.

Before answering me, she began rubbing her palms together, a nervous gesture I supposed, as if she were debating within about having this conversation with me.

"I was there with your mom in Rome, Quinn. I am not sure you are old enough to understand what happened."

"I-I'm almost 16. I . . . I understand more than you think," I replied, my voice tinged with shyness and a hint of fear.

"Do you know what happened to your mother?" She was now prodding me.

"She killed herself, Frances told me." I said. I was hoping she would believe that I was somewhat informed and believe that I was old enough to talk about such a serious situation.

"Quinn, I don't know why your mother decided to take her own life, or why Judge Barlow decided to announce it as a car accident rather than a suicide. He was doing what he thought was right for your family, I believe. She was sick, Quinn. She battled depression, and someday when you're old enough to understand this, I hope that you will have closure."

I could feel the tears welling up in my eyes. I rubbed them away and held back the truth. It was evident that Brooks had Susan as fooled as he did everyone else. I still couldn't come to terms with why my mother would leave me here with him. She knew what he was doing to me, to Miles.

"What I don't understand is where my mother's body is? She

had no casket. How did she do it?" I asked, becoming slightly irritated. Susan had no idea what I had endured, how much I had been through. I could handle this conversation. I just wanted answers.

Susan never reacted to my tone or my obvious display of frustration. She only looked up at me again and tussled her bottom around in the leaves before speaking. "You see, your mother drowned. She went into the ocean, and they assumed she was caught in a riptide. The beaches were closed for swimming that day, but she and I had already planned a day trip down to the beach at Lido di Ostia to take in the scenery. I had left to pick up lunch and she stayed back to set up our picnic. When I returned, her garments were on shore, but she was gone. I did not assume the worst initially. She never returned to the hotel later that evening, so I phoned the police. They found her watch on the bottom of the ocean floor, near where she had left her garments. She knew not to get into that water, Quinn. We were warned multiple times. She was different that trip. I could sense something was going on. I only thought the trip would help, improve her spirits."

I was crying again, but this time I couldn't wipe away the downpour, and the sleeves of my dress were saturated with tears. Susan moved in closer as I bawled, in what I believed was her attempt to console me. She began to desperately apologize, and I could tell she regretted telling me by the genuine sorrow upon her face and her now weakened posture as she sat with me beneath my tree.

Chapter Now

I CLEANED UP THE broken glass. Sam was back, licking my face as I stooped down with the dustpan and broom. I had lost my temper and unloaded my reality onto Miles selfishly. I did blame Miles; things could have been different for me had he stuck around. I hated admitting that I felt that way, and I liked to pretend to take accountability for my actions.

I washed off my makeup, regretting ever even putting it on. *What a waste,* I thought. *We aren't children anymore. Am I that naive to think that things would be the same between us? He isn't my knight in shining armor anymore. He isn't the Miles I once knew.*

I laid in bed contemplating my next move. I wanted the world to know what Brooks had done, but at what cost? It would destroy the beautiful life Kent had clearly built for himself, and he was expecting a baby, for God's sake. I knew his wife, Nora, would want answers even after all this time. I still wondered about my mother, and what really happened with her. I wanted to believe that the last time with her wasn't a goodbye, that she could never do such a thing. But she didn't protect me while she was here, and what makes this any different? The insanity made my head pound.

The next morning, I woke up consumed by an overwhelming urge, a magnetic pull back to the familiar embrace of my old habits. I knew the drill—I had learned techniques in therapy, like self-talk and logical reasoning, from Sherry. She painstakingly coached me on how to wrestle with these cravings, even crafting a list that I carried in my wallet for emergencies like this. Each item on that list was a lifeline, a vivid reminder of the bigger picture I desperately needed to cling to. It wasn't easy, but I managed to fend off the temptation, at least for now. Every moment was a battle, a fierce struggle against the allure of what I once sought solace in.

As I pulled into work, Claudia greeted me at the door with a smile. "Good morning, Quinn. How was your evening?" she asked.

I thought about telling her the truth about my evening, but I didn't. *How was my evening? You would not believe it if I told you, Claudia.* She didn't want the honesty; she wouldn't handle it well, I was afraid. "Noneventful, how about yours?" I answered back as I walked to the counter to retrieve my apron. She was following me, waiting for me to get my apron situated.

"Let me help you with that, darling" she said as she insisted on turning me around to tie my apron.

"Thank you, Claudia," I said as I grinned at her as I turned back around.

"Now, I have hired some more help, dear. Wedding season is upon us, and well, George's arthritis just can't manage it. Everett is an old friend of mine's grandson. Now, honey, he's not, well what do young ones call it—gay? He just needs a job, and I wanted to help Trudy out by giving him a job. He can deliver and such."

"Okay, Claudia, sounds good." I was a little confused and taken back by the amount and type of information she had just given me. *He isn't gay*, I repeated. Good to know, Claudia. As

I grabbed the stack of invoices covering my workspace, Claudia peeked around the corner once more. "Oh, and your visitor stopped by again early this morning, right before I opened up. Said she needed to talk to you about something important, I think that's what she said, honey. She said she would be back. She seemed to be in a hurry. Anyways, Everett will be in shortly. I will be up front waiting for him."

My visitor? Something important? Claudia had to have lost her mind. I didn't have any friends, so there was no one to come visit me. A mysterious visitor twice, though? It was unlikely she confused that, but she certainly could have been confused about the visitor's purpose. Before I had time to think about what Claudia had said, she rounded the corner with what I assumed to be Everett. He was younger than I expected, and surprisingly handsome—about my age, maybe a few years older. He wore a tattered T-shirt with the SCAD logo, Savannah College of Art and Design, written below.

"Quinn, this is Everett. Everett, this is Quinn," Claudia announced. Her voice was croaky, but not like a smoker's voice—like an older lady's voice, occasionally cracking as if her mouth were dry. She continued, "I have a couple up front to sit down with and discuss flowers for their nuptials, so I will leave Everett back here with you for a bit. Show him around if you don't mind, Quinn." She left the back hurriedly, leaving us standing there alone, gawking at one another.

"Well hello, Everett," I said as I cackled gracelessly right out loud. I wasn't sure why I giggled. There was nothing funny. "There is not much to show you. I mean, this is it," I said as I looked around, raising my hands in the air like I was presenting something spectacular. This time he laughed and scoped out the place before saying anything.

It was peculiar to find him attractive. Since Miles, I hadn't found anyone appealing and was still hesitant to trust men after what Brooks had put me through over the years. Yet, inexplicably, Everett felt comforting, his presence warm and demeanor gentle. His face exuded innocence. The pull toward him was both frightening and strangely thrilling. He didn't exactly appear safe; his muscular right arm was adorned with several tattoos, and despite his disheveled shirt and stained jeans, it was evident he took care of himself physically.

He stood tall, perhaps 6 feet, with dirty blonde hair falling over his forehead. He reminded me of a muscular Ryan Gosling, a nod to my love for *The Notebook*. While Everett examined the surroundings and gently touched the flowers, I glanced down at my attire. I was in joggers and a dreadful T-shirt, far less presentable than I realized. Thankfully, I had managed to apply makeup that morning, which gave me a sense of relief. I wasn't unattractive, I assured myself, resolving to take better care of myself. I inherited my father's smooth complexion, a stark contrast to my mother's lighter skin, and I had long legs and a slender figure. What more could I ask for, I concluded.

"How long have you worked for Claudia?" he asked.

"Not too long. I enjoy it. She is a charming lady, knows her flowers. She's becoming forgetful, through. She could use the extra hand for sure," I replied.

"You from around here?" he asked.

"You ask too many questions," I said as I laughed and handed him the shears. "You know how to use these?" I asked.

"Is the pope Catholic?" he shot back. I cackled again like a schoolgirl. "No, I don't, but you can teach me," he said as he moved closer and took the shears from my hand. His hand barely brushed mine, sending what felt like a jolt of electricity through me, catching me off guard.

It was pleasant though. I realized I had genuinely laughed and briefly disregarded the turmoil that overpowered my existence.

Human interaction was getting easier. I mean, it helped that he was spewing sensual vibes like water from a broken pipe.

I spent the day showing Everett how to use the shears, and he helped me work on the arrangements for delivery. He was a fast learner, and he even designed some arrays that put mine to shame. He was crafty, showing off his artsy skills. I learned that he was an art major that had dropped out about a year ago after difficult circumstances evolved. I didn't pry any further. Not on the first day, anyways.

Chapter **Then**

S USAN LEANED IN and hugged me one last time before disappearing towards the house. It was getting late, and the sun began to go down, beckoning me inside. I dried up and cleaned up my face as best I could. I was surprised that Miles had not come out to check on me, although I knew he had his hands full with Kent. The crowd had dwindled, leaving only a handful of people left. My radar was on as I entered, looking for Brooks in an endeavor to avoid him. I did manage to dodge him, and as I made my way to the stairs, I spotted Miles and Kent sitting on the third step next to one another playing some old handheld video game. Miles nodded invitingly at me as I approached them.

"I'm too old for this, I know," he said as he rolled his eyes at me. "You've been crying, are you okay?" he asked politely.

"I'm fine. We can talk later," I said as I looked over at Kent, absorbed intensely in his game.

"Kent, how ya doing? Whatcha playing there?" I said as I took a seat below them on the stairs. He ignored me and continued to play his game. Miles nudged Kent's shoulder, teasing him that he was also too old for that game too, but he was unbothered by our comments.

As the last of the visitors left, Brooks followed them to the door, shutting it behind them. We were still sitting on the stairs in his direct view as he turned around.

"Kent, go on upstairs, I'll be up soon" he said firmly, gesturing him upstairs to his room. Kent obliged and did as he was told. Miles and I stood up to follow.

"No, you two come with me. You wanted to see what's in the basement, so let's go take a look," he said sarcastically. *How did he know we had been in the basement?* I thought. I hung my head down even lower when I realized I had vomited on the floor and didn't have time to clean it up. He was the ultimate example of Jekyll and Hyde. He had depicted the perfect grieving son and husband all day long, and in a matter of seconds, converted to his real being, so full of anger and hatred, and I never understood why. He had money, power, and friends; he had it all, looking from the outside in. I guess the immoral just lived inside him. That's the conclusion I had come to, at least. As he unlocked the basement door I began to fidget, predicting his behavior. *Would he live up to his threat? I played my part, as I was expected. Did Susan tell him about our conversation?* The thoughts raced through my mind like a stampede of wild horses. I could tell Miles was doing the same thing, the lost look on his face. As we neared the end of the stairs, Brooks stopped to stare at the vomit. It was evident what it was.

"Who is responsible for this?" he asked without turning around. We stood behind him. I couldn't help but think about pushing him down the rest of the stairs and just running, running far away. Neither of us answered. He continued to walk, reaching the end of the stairs.

"What were you doing down here? And what were you looking for?" he asked once more in a sturdy tone.

Again, silence. By this time, he had moved closer to the

puke on the floor and was twisting his neck around as if he were stretching. We were both an arm's reach away from him. He began to walk to one of the shelves, grabbing a roll of paper towels and tossing it onto the ground.

"Clean it up," he said calmly. It scared me, his composure.

As we both knelt down to clean it up, Brooks suddenly kicked me hard in the gut, knocking the wind out of me. I collapsed, clutching my stomach in agony. From the corner of my eye, I saw Miles rise to his feet, his hand reaching for the bin where he had stashed the crowbar earlier. Brooks didn't intervene; he didn't know the crowbar was in there. As Brooks stood over me, seemingly relishing my suffering, Miles retrieved the crowbar and swung it at him. The first blow caught Brooks off guard, staggering him momentarily. Miles struck again and again, each blow driven by adrenaline, until Brooks collapsed beside me, blood streaming from a head wound.

My own adrenaline surged, and I managed to wrest the crowbar from Miles's hands. He stood there with a blank expression, his gaze fixed on Brooks, who lay bleeding on the ground.

I felt hysterically frantic, unsure what to do. I could feel my body shivering with fright, but it was as if I were hovering above the scene, my mind filled with flashbacks of Brooks's hot, stained breath on my skin. The sickness that swarmed my being each time he touched me. He was bleeding so badly that I knew we needed to call for help. As I reached down to get Brooks's cell phone from his pocket, I glanced over my shoulder to see where Miles had gone. I stopped as the memories of Brooks all over me engulfed me. I wanted him to die.

Miles sat at the bottom of the stairs, his knees drawn up to his chest, tears streaming down his face. It reminded me of the first time I had seen him cry, that night in his bedroom when he pushed me away silently. I hesitated, contemplating what might happen to Miles if I called for help. I couldn't bear the thought of him facing punishment for protecting me.

Stopping my search for the phone, I took a deep breath, a small sense of relief washing over me. I couldn't bring myself to dial 911. Sitting beside Brooks for a moment, I closed my eyes and imagined a life without his presence looming over us. Gathering my resolve, I stood and moved to sit next to Miles at the foot of the stairs, resting my head against his shoulder.

We sat there, never saying a word, only silence surrounding us. Brooks was no longer moaning or moving, so I assumed he was no longer alive. I couldn't look at him. I was still scared of him. Part of me was still terrified that he would leap up at any moment and charge at us, but he never did.

The rattle of Brooks' cell phone startled Miles and I, commanding us back into actuality. It was ringing and buzzing in his pocket as he lay there motionless in a large pool of blood. Miles stood up and moved calmly over to Brooks in search of the cell phone, powering it off after pulling it out of his pocket.

As he did, I began to tread up the stairs, exhausted and clouded, still feeling quite unsettled or unsure of our next move. I made my way up the stairs into the kitchen, alarmed to find Kent standing at the top of the stairs with a blank look on his face.

"Kent?!" I said as I swept the hair on his forehead out of his eyes, unsure if he knew what had transpired not long ago at the bottom of that staircase. As I waited for him to answer, I briefly glanced back down to see if Brooks's body was in his line of sight. It wasn't.

"I heard something earlier and I couldn't find anyone. Dad is not in his bed. Where's Miles?" he bashfully asked. His eyes were still swollen from that day, and he looked tired. He began to rub his eyes as if he needed to shut them.

""Everything's okay, Kent," I managed to say, my voice a little shaky as I guided him away from the basement door and toward the sink.

"Is that blood on you?" he asked, pointing to my arm. We stood in the kitchen, and I tried to maintain composure as I reached for a glass to fill with water. "Yeah, just a little nosebleed. I'm fine. Let's get you some water and then back to bed," I replied, attempting to sound nonchalant.

I kept it together as we walked to his bedroom. Sitting beside him on his full-size bed, I wrapped my arms around him and closed my eyes, silently replaying the terrifying events of the night, unsure of what to do next.

Chapter Now

I LEFT WORK THAT evening heading to the Hopeful House with so much still nagging on my mind, surprisingly, Everett mostly. I turned the radio on full blast, catching myself singing along to Adele, which was uncommon. It had been a long time since I really enjoyed music. I rarely even turned the radio on. It was like I didn't deserve the pleasure that music offered me. *Tragic.* I was still punishing myself for all my past endeavors, but this evening I did in fact enjoy the music, and it felt magical.

Everett was a breath of fresh air and a needed deflection. He was lively and charming. I wondered if he had a girlfriend, or a significant other that he was dashing home to. He was also mysterious; a lot like me, keeping the conversations light and amusing all day. Did he have skeletons in his closet like me? I found myself somewhat intrigued to find out.

I pulled up to the parking lot of the Hopeful House, and the lot was packed with cars. People were gathered outside the doors waiting to go inside. Most of the faces were familiar, but several I didn't know. I did not see Sherry, and I knew she had the key. Sherry was often late, nothing unusual. Punctuality was not her strong suit, but she always showed up. I sat in my car until I saw Sherry pull up and make her way to the door, letting the recovering souls flood through the door like a herd of cows seizing through the corral. I met Sherry at the door, as she spotted me walking from my car across the lot. "I'm glad you made it this week," she said with a grin. "Missed you last week."

"I know, I'm good, glad to be here," I said as I grabbed the door from her, letting her go before me. "And you're late," I sarcastically added as she briskly walked away turning her head and smirking at me once more.

I made my way to the coffee bar, making a black coffee and grabbing myself a homemade cinnamon roll, waiting for Sherry to beckon us to her safe circle. There were more people than usual tonight, I thought. As I waited and people-watched, Miles crossed my mind. He was angry at me, lashing out and acting out like a child throwing a tantrum. I had never witnessed his temper other than that night in the basement. The nights long ago when he grappled with Brooks, attempting to stop him, that was different, he was defending me. Those were acts of love and concern, not rage.

I settled into a seat near the back, next to an older woman I didn't recognize. She seemed uneasy, constantly shifting in her chair and gripping her purse tightly, as if it were a teddy bear or a grenade—I couldn't quite tell. Sensing her discomfort, I awkwardly extended my hand and placed it gently on her knee, offering a tentative smile. She glanced down at my hand, then up at me, slowly releasing her tight hold on the purse and placing it on the floor. I didn't utter a word, just greeted her with a warm smile that silently conveyed she was welcome to stay—and to my surprise, she did. I understood the sensation of feeling awkward and out of place.

As Sherry began to speak, the back door opened once more and in lingered another, a tall and handsome man that I immediately recognized. Everett.

"Everett, come on in and join us," Sherry said as she waved at him to take a seat.

I immediately began slouching low in my seat, trying to camouflage my existence and quietly praying he did not spot me. *How did Sherry know him?* I wondered. He was clearly a recovering addict just like me. It became clear to me at this point what the unfortunate circumstances were that he had spoken of earlier in the day. He was a user of some sort. *What are the odds,* I thought? *What awful heartbreak sent him onto this path?*

He didn't see me. I watched him from across the room as he sat in his seat, adamantly listening to Sherry and others' present stories and motivational speeches.

He had an undeniable magnetism about him, exuding a quiet confidence that was both intriguing and disarming. His demeanor was calm yet assertive, his movements deliberate and thoughtful. It was as if he carried a silent strength beneath his casual exterior, a strength that commanded attention without needing to demand it. As I observed him, I noticed how he interacted with others—attentive, yet not overly effusive, always with a hint of curiosity in his gaze. His presence seemed to suggest a depth of character that went beyond mere appearance, leaving me curious to unravel more about him.

I found myself puzzled by his situation; he appeared remarkably healthy, fit, and composed, as though he had taken excellent care of himself. Perhaps he was blessed with good genetics, or maybe his recovery mirrored Miles's, a graceful ascent from adversity. Thoughts of Miles flooded my mind, mingled with a hint of guilt for feeling drawn to another man.

After group, I could not disappear to my car fast enough, never giving Sherry the opportunity to catch me on the way out. I was almost certain Everett had not seen me. I wasn't ready to share my secret, and I was slightly perturbed that I knew his. I felt intrusive.

On my way home, I thought about Everett, trying to will the catastrophe called my life away, if only for a moment. It was odd to feel optimistic, but still lingering in the back of my mind was justice for all the victims taken by Brooks. The agony of living without answers was so familiar to me, like my mother taking her life without any explanation to me. Wondering all these years about why, never really feeling any resolution. I knew those families were desperate for answers just as I was. I knew I could give Kent's wife the closure she longed for. I recognized I needed to convince Miles to confess to what we had done, to clear my conscience. To let the world know what a monster Brooks really was. Of course, that came with the risk of being sent back to where I came from . . . and who would even believe me? I had no proof, but I suspected Miles did.

Chapter **Then**

I WOKE THE NEXT morning to Kent sitting on the chair beside the window staring at the sun, and I could tell by his flushed cheeks and reddened eyes that he had been crying again. I felt guilty and shameful, and sad for him. His life had changed so abruptly in a matter of a week, and he didn't even know yet that he would never see his father again. *His father*, I thought. I jumped out of the bed and rushed to Miles's room, leaving Kent sitting alone in his room. Miles was nowhere to be found, so I dashed down towards the basement, finding the door locked.

"Miles!" I shouted his name numerous times as I bolted wildly around the house in pursuit of him. The house was cold, all the drapes still closed and denying the sunshine entrance, making it even more gloomy than normal. The house was silent and still as I searched each room, unable to find Miles.

Miles was nowhere to be found, leaving me to spend the day with Kent, trying to maintain a facade of normalcy while my nerves were frayed. I found myself snapping at Kent, my patience wearing thin, though I knew it wasn't his fault. As evening approached and Miles still hadn't returned, my anxiety grew. I began to fear he had left, fulfilling his earlier threat to run away.

During dinner, Kent asked again about Miles and his father, and I concocted a story about them being out of town, promising they would return tomorrow, even though I doubted it myself. It was the best lie I could muster under the circumstances, my mind racing with uncertainty.

To distract Kent, I engaged him with games and television until bedtime. After he went upstairs, I attempted to pry open the basement door with a knife, but my efforts were futile. Part of me wasn't sure I even wanted to get inside, and the thought of what I might find there paralyzed me.

Throughout the evening, the telephone and doorbell incessantly rang, but I ignored them, convinced they were calls from Brooks's associates checking in after the tragic events. Each ring heightened my unease, amplifying the chaotic whirlwind of emotions inside me.

I needed Miles to return home. I was feeling extremely overwhelmed and on the edge of a nervous breakdown by the next morning. I didn't sleep at all through the night, and I had not eaten in over a day. I felt a knot in my stomach that would not subside, and my head was constantly swimming. I wasn't sure how long I would last in this condition. *Had Miles run away? Had he killed both Frances and Brooks and left me to handle Kent and this turmoil all alone? No, he wouldn't do that to us.* But 3 days had come and gone, and Kent was now aggressively persistent. He had finally stopped crying for his grandmother and his father, but the questions prevailed. As we gathered in the kitchen together, I felt my heart racing and the sweat pouring down my forehead. My hands were trembling so recklessly that I dropped the plate of food I had made for him. As the plate crashed to the floor, my chest tightened and I couldn't catch my breath. I was at another point of utter despair. I hit the floor hard, hitting my head on the barstool on the way down.

"Quinn, Quinn, are you okay?!" he screamed as he jumped up from his seat, kneeling beside me momentarily before running to the phone, finding it off the hook. I remained silently staring at the ceiling, thinking that maybe God would just take me, but I believed he wouldn't. He had abandoned me too. Kent dialed 911, and I didn't stop him. I didn't have the energy. As I lay there on the familiar tile, I thought about dying, being reunited with my dad and my mother. I thought about how much easier that would be. I wouldn't have to explain to anyone what I had let happen or answer any more questions from Kent. I decided then I was better off dead. But the ambulance came, rushing Kent and I to the hospital. On the way the paramedics informed me that I had had a panic attack and kept assuring me that I would be okay. It wasn't the news I wanted.

After arriving at the ER, the nurses obviously insisted on calling my parents. I explained to them that my mother had passed, but I gave them Brooks's cell phone number, knowing he wouldn't answer. After several hours and several attempts to locate him, CPS was called. It was standard practice for the hospital. I was, after all, still a child, and they couldn't very well let us hang around or send us home. I managed to choke down a pudding cup and a sprite, feeling slightly boosted, but nonetheless still drained. I could tell that one of the nurses recognized me. After all, I had visited this ER many times with "accidental injuries." Her eyes were tender, the way she looked at me, like she pitied me. Almost as if she knew something, like she felt sorry for me. But she said nothing. She carried on about her job as I waited for our caseworker to arrive.

Being we had the Barlow name, the caseworker arrived in no time. I told the lady that Frances had just passed away and that Brooks had disappeared shortly after without explanation.

I lied again, stating I wasn't sure where he had gone or when he would return. I shared with the caseworker that Miles had also disappeared, but she told me he was 18 years old and free to run off if he wished. She wasn't nearly as concerned with his whereabouts as I was.

That's when Elena showed up to take us home.

Chapter Now

S AM WAS HAPPY to see me, nudging me with his nose at the door waiting for me to grab the leash to take him outside. As we walked downstairs, my phone began blowing up. Sherry was calling, I was sure to ask why I had rushed out without saying goodbye. I let her go to voicemail. I secretly wanted to know more about how she knew Everret, but it would have to wait. As Sam began to pilfer around in the grass, I admired the trees, trying to distract myself from the constant urge to numb the pain in my being. The meetings sometimes stirred up reminiscences, some not so fond. The trees were calming, particularly this large one, big and strong framing amongst the sidewalks and complexes, reminding me of my tree long ago that brought me much-needed peace many times. Sometimes when it was hot, Sam and I would perch up against it and draw the shade while we watched our neighbors come and go like the sunshine.

"Hurry up, Sam," I murmured to myself while my own bladder felt like it may explode at any minute. It was late, and as I watched Sam examine every blade of grass, growing more impatient with his indecisive conduct, I spotted a pair of bright headlights turn into the parking lot. The lights drew closer, and

I realized the vehicle looked familiar. It was Kent in his squad car.

Kent parked and hopped out of his cruiser and began walking towards me, waving politely as he neared. He appeared expressionless with a blank look upon his face, worrying me immediately, unable to read his mood or the reason for his late-night visit.

"Quinn, what are you doing out here this late?" he asked in a soft, concerned tone, making his way to me. Sam ran over, welcoming the stranger with a friendly tail wag, begging for a head rub. Kent paid no attention to Sam, only continued to stare at me, waiting for my answer.

"Yeah," I said hesitantly. "What are you doing here, Kent?" I proceeded to answer, followed by a question of my own.

"I got a call from Miles. I was worried about you," he answered as he finally broke the uncomfortable eye contact to rub Sam's head briefly.

"Worried?" I could feel my head tilting to the side, wondering what he meant by that. "I'm sorry, what do you mean? I guess I'm confused. A call from Miles?" I questioned once more.

"I am just here to help, Quinn, please don't be upset," he said gently as he raised both hands as a gesture for me to remain calm, I assumed.

"Help? With what? What did Miles say to you?" The tone in my voice had inadvertently changed as I continued to sort out his last statement to me. *What had Miles said to him?*

"Can we go inside and talk?" he asked.

"I don't understand," I said once again, this time becoming slightly impatient and aggressive, now pushing Sam away from my legs. "What is going on, Kent? What did Miles say to you?"

Kent looked away for a moment before turning back around to reach for my arm. He was now lightly touching my arm. "He is only concerned about you. He said you have been talking crazy, said you threw a glass at him the other night. I want to help you, Quinn. I know you have been through so much already."

I ripped my arm away from him, feeling offended. "I am fine, and the concern? All of a sudden he is concerned about me? Well, I am not using, Kent, I am sober. I literally just came from a meeting." I felt like a small child battling to defend myself.

Kent took a few steps back, "Okay, okay. Can we just go upstairs and talk?" he asked once more.

I bent over to pick up Sam's leash, then placed the leash back on him. "No, we can't. I don't owe you or Miles any explanations. Why don't you grill Miles about what went down in our basement ten years ago, huh?" I retorted sharply, tugging Sam along with me.

Kent stood silently, observing as I marched back into my building.

Wow, Miles, I thought, *you are setting the groundwork in case I decide to let the world know what happened to me or what we did.* He was clever and manipulative, I'd give him that. It hurt my heart to know that he would betray me yet again. *Did he ever love me at all? Do I even know what love is?*

Chapter Then

THE POLICE CAME to Elena's house to interview both Kent and I numerous times in the next few days about Judge Brooks. Neither one of us had much to offer them about where he had gone. I would ask about Miles and if they knew where he was, but his absence seemed of no importance to them.

Elena eventually took us back to that house to gather some things so we could better settle into her home until Brooks was found. Walking back through the doors of the Barlow house sickened me. It was evident that the police had been here, because there were many things out of place. I could relax to some degree, assuming that Brooks was no longer lying on the basement floor. Undoubtedly, we would be aware had they found him. I was relieved that I would not be explaining to the police officers what had happened to him, and without Miles around to attest to it. *If they hadn't found him, where has his body gone?* I thought. *Did Miles return and move him out of the basement?* I had no idea, and frankly, I didn't care. I had grown so furious with Miles that part of me was glad he had to do it alone. Kent and I packed up what we could, never wanting to look back.

Elena lived in a nearby town and from what I gathered she and Brooks were not close. She was careful with her words, but when she looked at us, I saw sympathy in her eyes, as if she knew something, just like the nurse in the ER. *Did people suspect or even know what Brooks was or what he was capable of and just turned a blind eye to it?* Some nights I hated Elena thinking about it, my mind bogged down with suspicion. We never spoke of Brooks, ever.

Weeks went by without a word from the detectives. Kent and I returned to school as if nothing had happened. He adjusted well, surprisingly, and he and Elena appeared to have bonded fairly quickly. I, on the other hand, didn't trust her. I trusted no one and longed for an escape from my frustrations. My disappointment with Miles, my mother, Elena, the ER nurse—they had all let me down.

"Where have you been?" Nathan leaned on the locker next to mine, his voice low.

"Around," I replied, grabbing my notebook and shutting the locker.

Nathan followed as I walked towards class. "Yeah, so I heard about your dad going missing," he said unexpectedly.

I stopped in my tracks, feeling my face flush. "He isn't my dad, Nathan," I informed him firmly.

We stood there in awkward silence momentarily.

"Sorry, I just thought . . ." Nathan began.

"I'm fine. In fact, what are you doing tonight?" I interrupted, eager to change the subject. "I wouldn't mind disappearing," I added, waiting for his response, hoping he'd agree to hang out.

Nathan gently grabbed my shoulder. "You need to disappear. I can help you with that," he said, a slight smirk crossing his face.

"Today just blows, man, let's get the hell out of here now, what do ya say?" he asked as he looked towards double doors leading to the parking lot. "I have a car now, you know," he added.

That was the last time I went to school. I rarely even returned home, and when I did, Elena made no mention of it. She ignored the fact that I was rebelling. I really wondered if she even cared. Sometimes I would steal money from her purse and give it to Nathan for alcohol and drugs. I liked the way it made me feel, specifically the molly. The molly eventually led to cocaine, and Nathan began dealing, making it easily accessible to me. The euphoric high was undeniably my way of finding pleasure in my disastrous existence.

I didn't tell Nathan what had happened to me or what I had done, although we grew closer because of what now was an addiction. My days were now the same, wake up, get high, and drink, lost in conversion, leaving my tragedy behind—or so I convinced myself. The bustle of Brooks missing slowed down, and the town moved onto the next misfortune. After a year, I knew that Miles was officially never coming back for me, and it intensified my addiction even further.

My visits to Kent became less frequent over time. Elena, perceptive and caring, was keenly aware of my struggles, and often pulled me aside to express concern. She urged me to seek help, but I stubbornly denied any need for it, often leaving abruptly after our conversations. As tensions grew, I eventually stopped visiting Kent altogether, feeling unwelcome under Elena's watchful eye. Despite this, I found solace in knowing that Elena was there, providing Kent with the care and attention he needed.

Chapter **Now**

H OW DARE HE? I asked myself on the way back up to my apartment. The audacity to show up here all but accusing me of using again. And how dare Miles implicate to him that I was not okay? I was livid. I picked up my cell and attempted to call Miles. Straight to voicemail. *You coward.* That's okay. I would rather confront him in person with this anyhow, and I planned on doing just that, but for now I needed to lay down and attempt to recharge.

The next morning, my lack of sleep brought me to a groggy wakefulness. By this time, I had persuaded myself that I was defensive and irritated towards Kent the night before, and I felt remorseful for it. I had instantly blamed him for what could have been genuine concern instead of reassuring him like the adult that I was that I was in fact doing alright. I decided after work that instead of confronting Miles, I would make things right with Kent, and maybe even divulge my secret . . .

I managed to make my way into work. "Good morning, Claudia," I said as she greeted me at the door and followed me as I placed on my apron. She was energetic and happy to see me, which was soothing after such a crap evening. She was running through the list of to-do's noting that Everett would be in to help me by mid-morning.

"Okay, thank you, Claudia, I will get to it," I replied as I headed towards the back. "Oh, and your secret friend came by again this morning, she left you a note this time," she added. I froze and turned around; Claudia was holding a folded piece of paper in her hand. "She said to give you this."

I fetched the paper out of Claudia's hand and headed straight for the bathroom.

Dear Quinn,

I write this note in shame, regretful that I did not protect you. Please call me. I need to talk to you.

806-234-6790

Love, A

"Talk to me," I mused, staring at the message signed with an A. After all these years, what could she possibly need to discuss with me? As I stood there, gazing at my reflection in the mirror, the urge to call her right then and there surged within me. Anxiety flooded my chest, adrenaline raced through my veins, and a wave of nausea swept over me. I realized I had no one to confide in, no one to seek advice from. Miles, once significant, now felt distant and irrelevant. The loneliness weighed heavily on me, my stomach churning like a dryer in turmoil. I rushed to the bathroom, clutching the sink as vomit forcefully erupted from my throat.

"Quinn?" I heard the gentle tap against the door, catching me off guard. "You okay in there?" Everett asked.

"Yes, yes I'm fine, just a stomach bug, I think. I'll be out shortly."

I hurriedly cleaned myself up, dreading opening the door to face Everett after he had undeniably heard me upchucking.

I opened the door to find him standing a few feet away with a slight grin upon his face. "I got sick yesterday and puked on the elevator on my way home. It was disgusting on so many levels," he said as he continued to smirk.

I laughed. "Good one," I said as I rolled my eyes at him and pressed by him. He laughed along with me and followed.

"Seriously, you okay?" he asked genuinely. "I can go grab you a sprite or something. Is this contagious?" he added along with another sarcastic poke.

"I'm good, I'll be fine. I thought you weren't going to be here until mid-morning?" I said as I tucked the note deeper into my pocket, still preoccupied with what Anna wanted to tell me.

The nausea passed promptly, seeing as Everett was there to humor me. He was a delight to be around, and I noticed I felt at ease in his presence. For some reason he reminded me of my dad, illuminating with an appealing free spirit about him. The more conversation we explored, the more I felt safe in revealing my individuality, and possibly all my secrets. He was easy to talk to, a roll with the flow type lad. He seemed to exhibit an unjudging attitude, trusting himself and apparently living courageously.

Throughout the day, I held back from revealing my true thoughts, grappling with my feelings. Was I simply seeking someone to talk to, and he happened to be there? Or did I genuinely believe he could be the one to help me? Was my longing for companionship clouding my judgment? These questions swirled in my mind, unanswered.

"Well, Quinn, what do you think?" he asked. I was lost in my own thoughts, not hearing a word he had said. He was holding up a glass vase filled with Peruvian lilies.

"I think it's gorgeous," I responded, snapping out of my contemplations.

"Thank you, but what about dinner this evening?" He looked at me with a puzzled expression.

"Dinner," I repeated, then hesitated. I wanted to rush home, call Anna, maybe even visit Kent to apologize for my behavior the night before. Or perhaps confess the tragic truth about Brooks. "I'm sorry, I can't tonight. Maybe another night?" I answered, feeling torn.

Everett's brows furrowed slightly. "Another night then," he replied, a touch of disappointment in his voice. He paused, considering something, before nodding to himself. "How about Friday? There's a great little Italian place downtown. We could grab dinner around 7?"

I hesitated again, uncertain. Friday seemed so far away, and yet the thought of diving into Kent's world, confronting my past, was daunting. But maybe a normal evening out was exactly what I needed. "Friday sounds good," I finally said, surprising myself with the decision.

"Great!" Everett's smile returned, a hint of relief in his eyes. "Friday it is. I'll text you the details." He checked his watch and glanced around the office. "I should get going. See you tomorrow?"

Chapter Then

THE NIGHT TERRORS tormented me relentlessly, jolting me awake in unfamiliar rooms, disoriented and alone. Sometimes Nathan was there, a fleeting presence offering little comfort. Most often, I navigated this chaotic existence on my own, driven by the numbing allure of euphoria that dulled the looming consequences of my actions.

In rare moments of sobriety, Miles haunted my thoughts. I wondered where he had taken Brooks that dreadful night, whether justice would ever find its way to their dark secrets. Those thoughts consumed me, pushing me back to the only solace I knew could quiet them—a drink, a fix, anything to numb the pain and memories that clawed at me. And always, in the back of my mind, was the image of my father's disappointed face, a constant reminder of the person I was becoming, a stranger to the daughter he once knew.

Addiction expanded its grip beyond alcohol and drugs; it became the rudder steering my life. Emergency rooms became familiar territory, where I begged, bartered, and manipulated my way to temporary relief when money ran dry. Elena's refusal to fund my habits left me financially adrift, matched only by my emotional instability. The ER doctors, weary and overworked, often enabled my downward spiral, too exhausted to offer more than temporary solace.

I didn't stick around Beaufort. I was wandering, mostly with strangers. Nathan was arrested about 2 years after I stopped visiting Kent, and I made my way up to north Charleston. I felt alone and scared, as I really had since Miles had left me . . . until I met Lenny.

Lenny entered my life—a man twenty-two years my senior, with means beyond my grasp. I had taken a job at a seedy massage parlor known for illicit activities, barely scraping by until Lenny's arrival. Unlike other men, he was kind, respectful—a stark contrast to my usual clientele. Meeting him on my nineteenth birthday, I agreed to let him treat me to dinner after my obligations. With nothing to my name and a desperate need for stability, I moved in with Lenny, drawn in by the promise of a roof over my head and a steady supply of drugs. Lenny spoke little of his past, and asked even fewer questions about mine. Our arrangement was clear but unspoken—we existed in each other's orbits. Days hazed into nights as I became Lenny's full-time courier, ferrying his goods across town and beyond. His home, a haven from the harsh realities outside, offered a fragile sense of security in an otherwise chaotic world. I didn't love Lenny, but I clung to the stability he provided, the temporary reprieve from the tumultuous life I had led.

Time passed in the blur of deals and close calls, until one day at a private airport, the DEA swooped in on us. Lenny's secretive world fell apart under their investigation. Caught in their net, I had a tough decision—work with the authorities, share what I knew for a lighter sentence, or stand trial alongside Lenny, facing serious consequences.

Chapter **Now**

I LEFT THE FLOWER shop in a hurry, waving at Claudia on my way out in passing, trying not to be tangled up in chat before leaving. Claudia was a good woman. She reminded me often that there were still good people in the world. I was grateful for her kindness and normality. I regretted not taking Everett up on his dinner offer, but I had things to do before I lost my nerve. I decided to see Kent first. I was embarrassed at the way I had reacted the night before. I left the flower shop and headed towards Beaufort.

The drive was uneventful. I focused on the beauty in the scenery, the tall trees hovering below the darkness that blanketed the sky, the river fronts with old boats lining the bank. The sky was full of stars that evening, bright, calling for my attention, relieving some pressure I had placed upon myself about the approaching disgrace.

Before heading to the police station to find Kent, I drove my car to the old house, the place that haunted me. It was a house of terrors, where I lost my innocence and my ability to connect with others. It felt like I was compelled, not in control of my own body, needing to confront the monstrous dwelling where it all happened, treating it as a final farewell.

The old house loomed ahead, casting a sinister silhouette against the fading light of day. Its once grand facade was now weathered and worn, like the wrinkled face of a forgotten relic. The windows, boarded up and stained with grime, stared blankly out into the gathering dusk, refusing to yield any glimpse of the secrets held within. The encroaching tree line, now tangled and unkempt, seemed to encircle the property like a malevolent force, casting long shadows that danced eerily across the decaying structure. Despite its diminished state, the house retained an aura of menace, a lingering reminder of the nightmares it had once housed.

From my car, I stared at the house, bracing myself for the memories it held. This place, where innocence was shattered and trust betrayed, still loomed large in my mind. I parked my car by the driveway, unsure if I should step out. Was this closure, a final act of defiance before I unleashed my secret upon the town like a storm? As I looked at the once terrifying house, I suddenly felt liberated, no longer imprisoned by its memories. Empowered by this newfound freedom, I drove straight to the station without leaving my car.

Kent was not in the station, as I had expected, what with it being so late in the evening. I managed to persuade the lady manning the front desk to give me directions to his home. Small town folks were so trusting. Not shocking to me.

It was almost 8:00 p.m., and I supposed I would be interrupting dinner at the Barlow home, feeling somewhat remorseful for doing so. I presumed Nora had prepared a nice meal for her hardworking husband, not anticipating a visit from the estranged drug addict sister. The house was waterfront, small and cozy, just as I pictured it would be. I thought about the nursery they had likely organized, awaiting the arrival of a new baby. It suddenly became difficult to swallow, feeling a slight gurgle turn my tummy into knots.

I rang the doorbell; a lovely inviting tone graced the home as I stood there shaking, waiting for the door to open.

Nora opened the door, startled with a slightly puzzled look present upon her face. I could tell she recognized me.

"Hi, Nora," I said as I took a step back, trying to appear less menacing. "Is Kent here?" I asked reluctantly.

She remained frozen before snapping out of it and forcing a soft smile.

"Yes, um, yes, he is. I will grab him," she responded, her words stammering. She lightly closed the door, leaving me alone on the doorstep.

I undeniably caught her off guard, making me uneasy. She was always a nice girl, the good girl that I wished I had turned out to be. I could feel my breaths becoming heavy. I began to practice my mediation breathing. *In and out, Quinn, you got this.*

Kent appeared at the door, adjusting his shirt and taking a step out onto the doorstep to join me.

"Quinn," he stated, obviously surprised at my intrusion. "Listen, about last night, I'm sorry. I know I was presumptuous and forward, and I wasn't trying to be impolite. I just, well, I thought I should check on you is all."

"No, don't apologize, I overreacted. I am the one that needs to apologize. I was defensive and rude, and I am embarrassed by it. I came to reassure you that I am doing well. I am sober, honest."

"You could have called; you didn't have to drive all this way. Come in," he said as he pushed open the front door, signaling to me to follow him inside.

I hesitated to follow him inside, feeling extremely uncomfortable about dropping a bombshell in the company of Nora.

"Well, Kent, is there any way we could talk in private? I need to tell you something. Well—something that is difficult to say out loud, especially in the company of others."

Kent moved back out onto the doorstep once again, shutting the door firmly this time to be sure it was closed. He looked baffled as he gestured at me toward two rocking chairs on the porch.

We sat in silence for a moment while I gathered my thoughts.

"The stars sure are bright tonight. Awfully pretty," he said as he looked up at the sky, tilting his head as if he were making pictures out of the stars. He wasn't rushing me, and I was grateful.

"You know, I drove by the old house this evening. It looks surely different from what I remember," I said as I entertained the pictures in the sky with him.

He looked away from the sky and back at me, "Yeah, I have let it go, haven't I? I can't make myself get rid of it."

I pulled away from his eye contact, as we clearly did not share the same memories that developed in that house.

"Listen, Kent, that night . . . the night that Brooks disappeared. Do you remember anything?" I asked, my voice trembling as I struggled to form the words. I hesitated, feeling the weight of my secret pressing heavily upon me. For years, I had carried this burden alone, shielding Kent from the truth to protect him, or perhaps to protect myself from the consequences. The memory of that fateful night haunted me, its details etched into my mind like scars.

As Kent looked at me expectantly, I could see the innocence in his eyes, the trust he placed in me. He deserved to know, but I feared how he would react, how this revelation would reshape his world. Yet, I knew I couldn't keep hiding it any longer. It was time for the truth to come out, no matter how painful.

"I need to tell you something," I continued, my voice steadying slightly. "It's about what happened that night. Brooks . . . he didn't just disappear."

Chapter **Then**

THE STRIP SEARCH at the prison left me feeling shameful and dirty. There were two officers, a female and a male, though having a woman present did nothing to ease the humiliation. Officer Samson loomed over me, close enough that I could feel her breath on my face. She screamed at me to move faster as I reluctantly shed each garment, my hands shaking uncontrollably. Fear of the unknown ahead mixed with withdrawal pangs made the process agonizing.

Standing unclothed alongside six other women, all appearing as lost and devastated as I felt, I cupped my breasts, feeling exposed and vulnerable. Despite the mortification, I couldn't help but compare this moment to the horrors of the Barlow house. That place had left an indelible mark of filth and degradation on me, and this, however humiliating, seemed almost bearable in comparison. I reassured myself that if I had survived that, I could endure prison.

In my cell, my older cellmate remained silent and withdrawn during those initial days. She sat on her bed with closed eyes, rarely venturing out even for meals, as if struggling to accept her new reality. Some nights, I heard her stifled sobs and restless movements on the hard bunk, a poignant reminder of the emotional toll of confinement. The lack of sheets or covers on the beds seemed designed to prevent any desperate acts, further reinforcing the stark reality of prison life.

As I acclimated to this bleak existence, I clung to the fragile hope that my past resilience would see me through the challenges ahead. Little did I know then how much more I would have to endure in the days to come.

My new "home" was grimy, with a stainless steel toilet squatting in the corner and a meager amount of toilet paper haphazardly stashed behind it. The walls were dingy gray, marked with grime and scratches, showing their age and frequent use. I was now clad in an orange jumpsuit bearing the number 724 on the back. Compared to some places I'd slept, this was definitely not the worst.

Inside, tensions ran high among the inmates. Voices often escalated over minor disputes, echoing through the narrow corridors. I kept my distance, avoiding eye contact with the more aggressive ones. The guards were rough and loud, always on patrol with an authoritative air. Their constant presence reminded us we were closely watched, adding to the uneasy feeling that hung over the prison.

As the days passed, Helen and I started to get along. By the second week, we were talking, finding comfort in each other's company amidst the prison's grim atmosphere. We hadn't shared much about our personal lives yet, but her quiet support meant a lot.

One night, as I struggled with withdrawal, Helen sat next to me. She held my hair back as I vomited into the toilet. She didn't need me to explain; she understood the pain I was going through. Her silent presence and small acts of kindness began to create a bond between us, formed from our shared regrets and our battles with our own demons.

The cell was dark and cold one evening, and Helen sat up

from her bed and stood eye to eye with me while I lay on the top bunk bed. Her wrinkled hands clutched the bedframe, and she leaned in closer to my face as she whispered, "Honey, how did you get into this mess?" she asked so gently. Her voice was warm and genuine. All I could think about was that I wished in that moment I could disappear into the high, numb myself from the awful truth I was about to spew. The compulsion to detach was still haunting me, I couldn't seem to let it go.

I sat up in my bed as Helen climbed up to the top with me, sitting close making me feel slightly uncomfortable. She was at least 65, I guessed, looked as if she lived a hard life, not well kept, but I never suspected she was like me, a user. Her hair was short, silver locks hovering above her shoulders. Her skin aged her. Maybe she had spent time in the sun, I wasn't sure. But something had aged her.

"You've seen me going through withdrawals, Helen," I responded with a mix of shame and defensiveness. A single tear burned my cheek. "I'm a druggie; I was moving drugs and I was using drugs." My body fidgeted, feeling deeply embarrassed by her question and the vulnerability of the moment.

"But what happened to you? Something had to have happened to you, sweetie, to turn you to that," she asked curiously.

Helen and I bonded that night. She held me, fostering me like a mother. I was thankful to have her, letting it all go that evening. She was a hippie like my dad, interested in music and love stories. She had faith in me, convinced me that I could turn it all around. In the days, weeks, and year to come, she taught me to meditate. We would spend hours sitting cross-legged on the concrete floor, disappearing into dreams instead of drugs. It was an outlet I learned to cherish.

I never knew what Helen did to end up there with me. I never found the courage to ask. She was a moral person, so whatever it was, I decided she had to do it, and not out of hatred or evil. Whatever she did was to survive. Helen was my cell mate for 684 days before she passed away. She had a heart attack while she slept. I found her one morning as I attempted to wake her for our morning meditation. She looked peaceful, and I knew she had gone to a better place. She had, for the most part, motivated me to sober up and imagine a new way of life for myself when I got out.

I was never given a new cellmate after Helen's death. I was now at peace with the solitude, although I did miss Helen. The solace gave me time to sort out and plan my future, as Helen had encouraged me to do. I had thought of her as a friend, almost a mother.

Chapter Now

K ENT SAT UP straighter in his chair as he turned to look at me, almost as if he were troubled by my ask. His face tightened; I had clearly struck a nerve with my question. As I turned around briefly to gaze at the window to his home, I caught Nora abruptly shut the curtain when she saw me.

"Kent, I'm sorry, I know that night was tough on you as a child, losing your father. I'm sorry, it's just something that happened that night. Something that altered me, and Miles."

"I don't remember much, Quinn. I mean, I remember missing my dad, wondering where he had gone," he said as he seemed to relax a bit starting to rock back and forth again in the rocking chair, looking up at the sky once more.

"Do you realize what was happening in that house? To me?" I asked sharply, holding back tears. I could hear the tone change in my voice.

"My dad was a good man" he said frankly looking over at me, halting his rocker.

I froze temporarily, attempting to gather confidence within to continue my account and free myself from the guilt.

"I'm sure in your eyes he was. In my eyes, he was a monster.

You were just a little boy, Kent, unaware of what he was doing, what he did to me, and to all those others. Miles knows too. He was there, he saw what I saw."

I could tell I was upsetting him; his eyes grew darker and firm, his demeanor had quickly changed. It was clear he believed Brooks was a good man.

"What do you want, Quinn? Money?" he asked snidely. His arms were now crossed, and he was becoming impatient and frustrated with our conversation. "What did you want to tell me? Just say it already. He hurt you. Did my dad hurt you? Is your life a result of something my father did to you? He made you become a drug addict, whoring yourself out, leaving you no other choice?"

I remained silent, stunned by his comment. I waited for an apology to follow.

He was now peering at me, angry. How dare I show up accusing his righteous God-fearing father of indecency. This was not the Kent that showed up to my apartment, caring and gentle. This was a Kent I was not familiar with.

I finally countered, "No, Kent. My addiction, my problems— they're on me. I chose that path, and I've been dealing with the consequences ever since. But there's something else I need to tell you. Brooks . . . he abused me, Kent. It started when I was young, and I didn't know how to tell anyone. It's been haunting me all these years."

"What?!" Kent shouted, towering over me with irritation and annoyance. His body tensed, as if he were facing a grizzly bear. I felt feeble and weak under his gaze, but I knew I had to tell him the truth.

"I . . . Miles killed him," I blurted out, tears streaming uncontrollably down my face. "He hit him in the basement, and he died." Cupping my hands over my face, I struggled to conceal my shame and sorrow. "I did nothing. I should have called 911, but I didn't. I let him die. I wanted him to die. I wanted him to stop."

Kent started laughing. He was laughing. He looked at me like I was crazy. I took my hands from my face and stood up feeling clouded and a little dizzy, taken back by his reaction.

"You are crazy. Miles was right. The drugs really did you in, Quinn," he said nonchalantly as he shook his head in suspicion. "Don't you dare try to ruin Miles's life, you hear me?"

The dizziness persisted; I felt like a panic attack was nearing. *I heard him wrong.* I was sure. "What?" I asked uncertainly, hoping that I heard him wrong.

"Miles didn't kill our father, Quinn. Why in the hell would you even say that? Just stop it. Stop it now."

"Kent! Yes he did, I was there! I watched it happen. Miles hit him; we left him there!" I pleaded with Kent to believe me. I was now pacing the porch, again catching Nora peeking out of the curtains again. I'm certain she had heard our conversation grow louder and more intense. I ignored her and turned again to Kent. "And he killed Nora's sister, Brooks did. He had a box full of photos, photos of those girls found at Albergotti Creek. Miles saw them too!"

"You know what, that's enough, Quinn. You need to go," he said sternly as he pointed to my car. "Go. This is insane, you are insane. You need help. Miles warned me."

I was still sobbing, "Miles lied to you, he killed your dad!" I spurted frantically as I stepped off the porch and onto the walkway.

"Go home, Quinn. You need help," he said as he turned away from me and walked through his front door, slamming it behind him.

Chapter **Then**

RELEASE DAY HAD finally come. I had decided to relocate to Savannah, since my dad always spoke so highly of it. I could start over there, just as Helen and I had discussed so many times. It wasn't easy, but my case worker had set up my bank account, which held my inheritance and life insurance beforehand, so I was met with plenty of money for a new beginning. The first place I went after my release was to the animal shelter. I needed a companion. I felt catapulted into a new world, and I decided I needed a dog. That's where I met Sam.

I debated reaching out to Helen's daughters, or Anna, or even Miles, to seek guidance and support. In the end, I chose not to. None of them had visited me, and it didn't seem fair to expect them to look after me now.

Hopeful House became my new foundation, and Sherry my new Helen. She greeted me warmly on my first day, her smile genuine and her demeanor reassuring. Sherry understood the struggles, the relentless urges that never truly disappeared. She guided me with patience and empathy, teaching me strategies to manage my cravings and stay focused.

We connected instantly. I found solace in meditation and

spent time walking Sam, establishing a routine that grounded me. The weekly meetings with fellow recovering addicts were both challenging and uplifting. Sharing our stories was cathartic, reminding me of the depths I never wanted to revisit.

Sherry's approach was encouraging, tailored to my needs. She saw beyond the addiction, acknowledging the pain and the progress. Together, we navigated the highs and lows of recovery. Some days were draining, steeped in the heaviness of shared struggles, but they reinforced my determination to move forward.

At Hopeful House, I found not just sobriety, but a community that understood and supported me. Sherry's guidance was pivotal, her belief in my ability to heal unwavering. Each day became a step towards reclaiming my life, away from the darkness that once consumed me.

Sometimes Lenny would cross my mind. I wondered what had become of him. Was he still in prison? Was he angry at me? Would he retaliate someday? My past was shocking and filthy, and so I steered clear of making real friends or relationships. After all, who could love someone like me?

Claudia hired me on the spot at the flower shop. She was desperate for help, it seemed, or maybe it was just perfect timing. I enjoyed working for her. The flowers were tranquil and lovely, always making me feel cheerful. I was off to a good start, with a fresh beginning. I could reinvent myself here for sure. My apartment was more than adequate. I did splurge a bit on it, agreeing to myself that I deserved it for the fresh new beginning.

It wasn't until the news in Beaufort, the bodies, that I began to really second-guess the new me, remembering the life I had run away from. The guilt I felt knowing what I knew. *Am I really the new person I believe myself to be letting this go unsolved, not shouting from the rooftops what Brooks did to me as well?* That is when things really changed for me. I needed to be courageous, and after running into Miles amid it all, it was like fate. I could never really be the new me without acknowledging what we did and what we knew.

Chapter Now

I SAT IN MY car in front of Kent's house wailing like a baby for a good twenty minutes before making the trip back home. I wasn't thinking straight. I needed to get to my safe space. I needed Sam to console me as I walked through my door. I don't remember the drive home, but just as I wished for, Sam was there at the door to comfort me, the only sense of calm I had felt in the last few hours. I immediately felt safer, somewhat relaxed in his presence. I attempted to gather my thoughts and begin to evaluate what had just happened as I walked Sam down. I knew he was bursting at the seams to go outside by now. Sadly, he was all I had.

As I waited at the elevator with Sam, I recalled Kent standing there on his porch, proclaiming that I was a liar, and I was certain he believed I was still using. *Miles is trying to make him believe I'm crazy, covering his tracks. Where does he think his father is? He really believes he disappeared into thin air?* The questions assaulted me over and over, like a bull chasing seventy-eight red flags in the arena. The audacity. Miles was willing to throw me under the bus so that I couldn't squash his perfect reputation and rattle his perfect existence. He told me to let it be, and now I knew why.

Sam took care of business rather quickly, and we headed back up. He snuggled me extra tight that night like he knew I needed it, embracing me like I was his last breath. I slept terribly, dreaming of Brooks. I dreamt of him coming for me, confronting me, threatening me. I woke in a cold sweat, getting up and turning on every light in my apartment. I felt scared and livid all at the same time.

The next morning came, bearing sunshine through the blinds. I got up to turn off all my lights only to find Sam sitting at the front door, anxiously waiting for a walk downstairs to the grass. "Give me a minute, Sam, I'm coming," I said to him as I made my way throughout the house, finally arriving at the coffee pot. I felt tired and shaky, like I had been starved for days and then hit by a train. The real nightmare was waking up to the reality of what had occurred last night. *This cannot be happening,* I thought. *What now? Do I go on about my life like it never happened?* I felt beaten and defeated, the story of my life.

Just as I reached for the doorknob to take Sam downstairs, my phone buzzed. It was a number I didn't recognize. Apprehensively, I answered, "Hello?"

"Hey friend, want some coffee?" I heard Everett's soothing voice bellow out so cheerfully.

"How did you get my number?" I asked curtly.

"Good morning to you, too. Claudia gave it to me. Now, do you want some coffee? I am leaving the gym and I thought I'd pick us up some on the way to work."

"Work, shit," I hollered out. I hung up on Everett briskly and hurriedly rushed Sam downstairs to potty before running back upstairs to throw on some clothes for work. My mind wasn't right this morning. I had too much going on. Work was the only stable thing I had in my life, and I certainly didn't want to lose that.

Everett met me at the door, handing me my apron. I was ten minutes late, but Claudia didn't seem to notice.

"You okay?" Everett asked skeptically as he followed me to the back, wrapping my apron around me. He handed me a cup of coffee and stood in front of me like a puppy waiting for a treat or a "good boy."

"Thank you for the coffee and the morning call. It was a long night, but I'm okay." I was distracted, with an empty feeling in my gut, noticing that my tummy was growling rather forcefully.

"You don't look good. Another stomach bug?" he joked. This time I laughed. He could sure make light of a situation, which was comforting in the state I was in. "When is the last time you ate, Quinn?"

"How many orders do we have this morning?" I asked, completely ignoring his comment.

"Quinn, I'm serious. Are you alright?" This time he seemed intense, no smile or grin to follow. Was my distress that visible?

"No, I am not okay, I am not okay at all. I'm broken, everything is broken," I responded, automatically opening the flood gate and releasing a waterfall of tears.

He wasn't ready for that. He grabbed a box of tissues from the counter, handing them to me before stuttering, "I—I didn't mean to make you cry, I'm sorry."

I mopped my face up with the tissues. "You didn't make me cry. Don't apologize, please," I said as I then wiped the snot emerging from my nose. "I have an ugly cry, huh," I said as I halfheartedly laughed, attempting to deflect my embarrassment.

"Kind of," he said as he smirked at me and moved in closer. "Can I hug you?" he asked. I didn't have time to answer before he grasped hold of me and pulled me in. I buried my head in his chest. It felt shaped and strong, leaving me feeling protected for a short time.

As I continued to sob into his chest, I opened my eyes to

look up at him, afraid I would find a set of desperate wide eyes wanting to flee from my madness but instead he placed his hand under my chin, softly holding it, while he gazed at me sincerely. I was blinded, the moment was like a warm blanket splattered with bullet holes. Everett was trying desperately to wrap me up and relieve me, and I was undecided if his timing was good or bad.

Chapter **Now**

THE MOMENT ITSELF was comforting, the way he peered down at me while I wept, pretending that someone cared about me, that I had someone to share my troubles with. Still frozen in his arms, he leaned down, his presence gentle and reassuring, as if he wanted to offer solace without words.

I closed my eyes, feeling his closeness, his steadiness against the storm within me. His touch was calming, his presence offering a brief respite from the chaos. It wasn't just physical; it felt like a spiritual connection, a moment of shared understanding.

When he finally stepped back, pressing his forehead against mine in silence, the sound of the front door abruptly brought me back to reality. I gently pulled away and hurried to the bathroom, needing a moment alone to gather myself.

The day persevered and I dried up my tears. Everett and I did not talk about the kiss. We worked as if nothing had happened. I declined to talk about what was wrong, promising to have dinner soon to discuss my muddled life with my new admirer.

Claudia asked me a few times if I was okay. I lied to her, telling her my allergies were acting up. She bought my story, or at least she pretended to.

By lunch my body craved food severely, and just as a knight in shining armor would do, Everett picked up lunch and managed to carry most of the workload for the rest of the day. He watched me like a vulture, making sure I ate every bite of my sandwich and pasta plate.

Thankfully, for the most part, my mind was preoccupied with the orders for the day, and the kiss was an added bonus, but my mind did persist to wander a bit. I thought about Kent, about Miles and Brooks, and about Anna. *Did Anna know something? Was I crazy? Did I really see what I believed I saw that night? Could she help me?* I knew I needed to make that call, and I planned on doing just that, later. Work that day was surprisingly just what I needed to jumpstart a clear head.

"Can I take you home today?" Everett asked as we cleaned up and prepared the shop for tomorrow.

"I have my car, I can drive. I'm feeling better, I guess I just needed a good cry and a good lunch." I put on a good front and stood up tall when I answered, like I had conquered all my demons that day.

Everett wasn't buying it. I could tell by the smug look on his face as he stared me down while I removed my apron and grabbed my purse to leave. I wasn't exactly sure I fully trusted him, or anyone at that point. I mean, why did he care about me? Why did he kiss me? He didn't even know me. I had almost decided by the end of the day that he felt sorry for me. We said our normal goodbyes and left the flower shop as usual.

On the way home I stopped in at the corner store for dog food before arriving at my apartment complex. I had a terrible sensation charge my body as I got out of my car and headed up with the huge bag of dog food. It was a gut feeling of dread that I couldn't shake. I was also feeling remorseful that I had forgotten to order Sam's special food this week. With everything I had going on, it had slipped my mind, so dog chow would have to suffice, and Sam wouldn't be happy. The bag was heavy, and as I departed from the elevator, someone grabbed the bag from me and I couldn't tell immediately who it was.

"Miles! Jesus, you scared me." He had caught me off guard, effortlessly handling the bag better than I had. "What are you doing here?" I asked, my tone laced with irritation.

"Hello, Quinn. We need to talk. Kent told me you visited him." His voice sounded demanding. He was heading towards my door with the dog food over his shoulder like he was coming in whether I gave permission or not.

I dug my keys out of my purse, hearing Sam scratch at the door, eagerly awaiting my entrance. I let Miles follow me in. He greeted Sam like he knew him, which irritated me even more. I snapped at Sam, yelling at him to go on. His tail tucked and he headed towards my bedroom.

"Where do you want this?" Miles asked.

"Just set it down there," I spat, unable to control myself. Before I knew it, I was yelling at him, waving my hands wildly in the air. "You told Kent I was using? What the hell?!" The words erupted from me like a twisted tornado tearing through a town. Heat flushed my face, spreading down my neck and chest, overwhelming me.

"Listen, Quinn, I didn't know what to do. I warned you to leave it alone!" he exclaimed. "Why are you doing this?" He took a breath, unknowingly still holding the bag of dog food on his shoulder. "What is it that you want?" Tears gathered in his eyes but failed to descend, his expression sincerely apologetic. "Quinn, please." He finally dropped the bag of dog food to the ground, pulled out a chair, and plopped down into it. He placed his elbows on the table, gripping the sides of his temples firmly, massaging them—a habit from childhood that he seemed to still have.

"You left me there alone, to clean up that mess," I stated as I slammed my hand on the table, insistent on his attention.

"Stop," he said quietly as he began reaching for my hand. "I didn't know what to do."

I let him take my hand. I could see the pain in his eyes, his pleading was honest. He was lost then too, just as I was, his tears finally descending his cheeks and onto the table as he continued to clinch my hand.

"Miles, what happened? I mean, his body, it was gone. You cleaned up and just left. I mean, I thought you had come back and moved his body, the pictures, all of it."

He stared at me, processing what I had said. "Let it go. It doesn't matter. Please. We have a chance to start over. YOU can start over." He was now seemingly talking out loud to himself. "We were stupid, just kids," he mumbled to himself repeatedly. "We were just kids, you were just a kid. I was trying to protect you."

"But why? Why would you leave me there alone, after what you did?" I asked. I was baffled, stumped beyond reason, asking out loud without really expecting a convincing response. Miles was no longer crying, his arms had relaxed, and he was now slumped over the side of the table, both arms extended onto the table staring off into space like he didn't know what else to say to me.

My head was spinning with questions and frustrations. I reached over and grabbed his hand, squeezing it tightly. "Miles," I began sharply, my voice tinged with anger "I can't believe you persuaded Kent into thinking I was using again."

He looked at me earnestly, his expression pleading for understanding. "Quinn, I was trying to protect you. Kent was digging into things that could have made everything worse."

"Why are you so dead set on keeping all this secret? You were protecting me. It was an accident, right? Right?" I retorted, pulling my hand away sharply. "Instead, you went behind my back and made things more complicated, convinced Kent that I'm a crazy drug addict."

Miles sighed heavily, his shoulders slumping. "I know. I'm sorry, Quinn, I was scared."

"Scared?" I scoffed, feeling the sting of betrayal. "Miles, it was an accident. Why can't we tell the world what he did? I don't understand. You and I . . . he hurt us."

He reached out tentatively, his voice softening. "Quinn . . ." he paused.

I hesitated, still feeling raw from his actions. I softened my voice, "There are families out there that have no idea what happened to their loved ones, like Kent's wife."

He looked down, hurt and regret evident in his eyes.

I stared at him, torn between anger and the warmth of his touch. Slowly, I allowed him to pull me closer. His arms wrapped around me, and for a moment, I let myself lean into his embrace.

His breath brushed against my stomach, his face buried against me. His heartbeat echoed mine, both of us burdened by guilt and remorse. This was the side of Miles I yearned for, the one who could provide solace despite the chaos he had caused.

"I hate what you did," I murmured, my anger fading into resignation. "But I understand why. You thought you were protecting me."

He held me tighter, his touch comforting yet tinged with regret. "I'll do whatever it takes to make it right, Quinn. I promise."

I closed my eyes, feeling conflicted yet strangely reassured in his arms. Despite everything, I wanted to believe that his intentions were rooted in concern for me. For now, that realization softened my anger, if only slightly.

Chapter **Now**

I FELT A SURGE of guilt. It was the first time I had allowed the Miles I once knew, the Miles from my childhood, to exploit my vulnerability. After agreeing to let him stay over, we found ourselves sharing my bed amidst the aftermath of our argument. This was a significant moment, the first occurrence of such intimacy between us. There was a desperate need for a break, but instead of taking one, we slept together, a tumultuous blend of anger and love. Sometime in the night, Miles crept away, leaving me alone with a slight tinge of regret for giving in to him. It was the first time we had ever been intimate with one another, the first time our bodies had collided. I could still smell him in my bed and feel his grip around my thighs wrapping as he clasped me tighter and tighter. I had had sex before, but never this way. This was different. It meant something, I never loved anyone like I loved Miles. The way he navigated my body like a road map was something I had never experienced. The reminiscence made me tremble, leaving me absorbed in the memory. I had anticipated that encounter with him for almost my entire life. Still, part of me felt somewhat regretful, although I enjoyed every moment of it—but for some reason, I could not stop thinking of Everett.

"Sam!" I yelled as he jumped on top of me, licking me in the face, hurtling me back to actuality. "Get off!" I shouted as I pushed him off the bed and onto the floor. " Jesus, Quinn, what have you gotten yourself into now? Just when things couldn't get worse, you managed to throw some gas on the fire." I rebuked myself right out loud.

I rolled myself out of bed to take Sam out and make my coffee, inadvertently searching for a note around the house that Miles may have left. Nothing. I checked my cellphone for voicemail. Nothing. *Am I that naive, to think it meant something, to think it could be the beginning of us?* I let the thought rest as I showered and headed out the door to the flower shop to work. *Stick to normalcy,* I told myself as I craved a drink on the way to work, momentarily entertaining the thought of stopping into the corner mart for one small bottle. I could dump it into my water bottle, and no one would ever know. I didn't, though. I drove past the corner mart, never stopping.

The remainder of my drive, I thought of Anna again, and her note. I had not called her last night like I had planned. Miles threw a wrench into that plan showing up unannounced and somewhat seducing me. It was easier to blame him than take responsibility, and I had no energy to dwell on it this morning. I decided I would call her tonight after my meeting.

Everett was singing in the back when I arrived at work, his voice echoing through the shop as I opened the front door and made my way to the front desk to grab my apron. He peeked his head around the corner, broad shoulder visible.

"Good morning, Quinn, I brought you coffee," he said cheerfully, giving me a wink before disappearing back around the corner.

"Your thoughtfulness doesn't make this easy, you know," I murmured to myself as I headed to the back, unsure if he even heard me.

He stood in the back wearing a tight white T-shirt that hugged his arms and chest delightfully. "Doesn't make what easy?" he asked, his tone teasing.

"Nothing," I said, rolling my eyes and taking a sip of the coffee he had left for me.

"No, make what easy? You like me, don't you?" he quipped, picking up a bouquet of daisies and playfully dusting my face with them.

"I don't like you," I replied mockingly, watching him dance along to his own karaoke concert. Despite his job at a flower shop, he exuded a vibrant energy, settling on a champagne cloud despite life's difficulties. He embodied the kind of happiness my cell mate Helen had encouraged me to find.

"Are you taking medicine?" he asked as we loaded flowers into the delivery truck.

"Huh?"

"You keep checking your phone. Are you taking medicine or waiting on a call?" he inquired, closing the back and tapping it to signal George they could take off.

"I'm not checking my phone," I said snidely, pulling it out to stare at the screen, secretly hoping for a missed call from Miles. He laughed and shook his head as he walked back inside, with me following.

"I'm waiting on a call, but it's none of your business," I admitted, smiling at him from across the room.

"From whom?" he probed.

"Again, none of your business. Why are you so interested in who's calling me anyway?" I couldn't help but smile; we were playing a childish game, and I found myself enjoying it. "Where did you get all those tattoos?" I asked playfully.

"And now who's being nosy?"

"You wanted to play trivia, you go first. Why did you quit school and end up here, working for Claudia? You're clearly a genius," I said cynically, gathering flowers from the freezer, intentionally avoiding eye contact.

Silence filled the room. I sensed tension building. Turning around to apologize, I found Everett standing directly behind me, startling me into dropping a vase of roses, scattering glass across the floor.

"Shit!" I exclaimed as we both knelt to clean it up. As I began picking up glass, Everett stopped me, taking my hands into his. He gazed deeply into my eyes, open and ready to share something significant.

"You really want to know?" he asked softly, both still on our knees.

"If you want to share, I want to know," I replied earnestly. He seemed unburdened by shame, ready to confront his past openly.

"I got most of these tattoos in prison, Quinn," he said without hesitation. "You see, I made some damaging decisions that changed my path."

He continued, his palm sweating against mine. The room suddenly felt stifling. I panicked and stood, pulling my hands away from his.

"I made the choice to drive under the influence, risking not only my own life but my brother's as well. I caused his death, Quinn, because of my own recklessness and stupidity." He stood upright before me, his face suddenly overtaken by a wave of sorrow and regret. It was the first time I had seen him so vulnerable, so defenseless. This glimpse revealed that he, too, was wounded, bearing scars unseen to the casual observer. You had to look deeply to notice them.

Chapter **Now**

HIS CONFESSION SHOOK me. I didn't know what to say to him. I wanted to shame myself and expose my own secrets to make him feel better, but I didn't.

"I don't know what to say, Everett. I'm sorry," I said timidly. I had no idea what response was truly appropriate for his recent revelation, so I decided to dodge it for the time being, planning on delving in deeper at dinner, if he accepted. "You know, I wouldn't mind dinner tonight? I mean if you want to talk more?"

Truth be told I was just plain awkward, spending so many years messed up, and then prison, I was socially unsatisfactory, and I was well aware of it. I was twitching as usual when I got nervous, and I stooped back down to pick up the glass I had broken, to keep my hands busy. I genuinely felt bad for him, but I didn't know what to do for him. I was not as generous as he was to me in my time of need. When I finally looked back up at him, he seemed lighter, like he had released a beast and was set free. Like he was pardoned with admission of guilt, I supposed. He had picked up another vase and seemed to have already moved on.

"I can do dinner," he said as his phone began buzzing in his pocket. "Excuse me," he said as he dug into his pocket for his phone. "I am going to grab this call." He gently smiled down at me as he hurriedly walked away heading towards the restroom. *Thank goodness. Saved by the buzz,* I thought.

"Gracious! What happened here, Quinn!?" Claudia bellowed out as she walked into the back, never stopping, only stepping over my mess, clearly looking for Everett. "Where's Everett? I need him to move a heavy fern around the front for me," she shrieked.

"I'm right here," Everett replied as he emerged from the restroom hallway, tucking his phone back into his pocket as he followed Claudia to the front. He gave me a sly look as he passed me, softly grazing my shoulder, an obvious attempt to make me feel at ease.

I sat there on my knees, wondering what that felt like. To be transparent, unashamed. To own your truth. He wasn't proud of it by any means, but he had clearly come to some sort of peace with it. *I am a fraud,* I thought. I had been running from my truth for so long. I had this split-second clarity of future me, not running away from this darkness, but lighting my own candle. *Am I capable?*

I cleaned up my mess and finished my orders for the day, with heavy thoughts once again consuming me. I assumed Claudia had Everett doing some honey-dos for her or running errands, which was perfect for me. I was also thinking about how to renege on dinner, as I was stressing about what to wear once again; I had no options. How little this stress seemed to be in comparison to my big picture of reality, but nonetheless, I felt stressed. I was also thinking about Anna, Kent, Miles, Brooks, all the loose ends I needed to take care of but managed to run out of time for every single day. *I'm stalling, not running out of time. I know it.* And, well, I also didn't want to miss another meeting at the Hopeful house tonight. Sherry just might show up on my doorstep if I did.

My phone never rang. Miles never called me. I was not even sure I expected him to, but it was still disappointing. The night we had shared, then nothing. *What an asshole.*

By closing time Everett had reappeared to help me close up the place. He was his normal pleasant self, humming along to some light background music Claudia had turned on throughout the day, never appearing as if he had disclosed an extremely sensitive life event just hours earlier.

"Where are you taking me for dinner, Quinn?" He had indeed not forgotten. He was not going to let me back out of this like I had hoped. He removed his apron, signaling for me to hand him mine. *Was he missing a meeting too?* I wondered.

"Let's see," I scanned my brain for options. I was a hermit and I had no idea where to take this man to dinner. "You like Italian?" I asked.

"I sure do."

"Italian it is!" I said as I faked my enthusiasm. We agreed to meet at the only restaurant that popped into my head under pressure, which was, coincidentally, where Miles had taken me before. It would definitely be bizarre, but I was used to bizarre at this point.

I drove home to let Sam out and get changed, and as I walked back upstairs with Sam, my cell rang from a blocked number. I answered, thinking it could be Miles calling from the hospital.

"Quinn?" the voice shuddered.

"Who is this?" I responded.

"It's Anna. I need to talk to you."

Chapter Now

"ANNA?" I COULD hear the shock in my own voice as I said her name aloud. Silence filled the other end briefly before I heard a slight sigh of relief, and then she began to speak.

"Can you meet me?" Her voice sounded as if she were whispering or scared. I couldn't tell.

"Now?" I answered her. I felt strange, trying to understand what she could possibly need to tell me so hurriedly now all these years later.

"Yes, now. Meet me at Crate Park near the yellow slide in 1 hour." She didn't give me a chance to respond before hanging up.

Sam and I entered the house. I could barely free his leash from his collar because my hands were shaking so abrasively. *Why was I so tense. I wanted to talk to Anna, she was always an ally to me, she was so good to me long ago before disappearing, before being pushed out by Brooks.*

Before I knew it, I was out the door, heading to the yellow slide in Crate Park. Everett didn't cross my mind until I passed the flower shop on my way. *SHIT. I'm sorry, Everett.* I shook my head in disappointment at myself. My nerves were shot, and

I didn't have the energy to even call and explain myself to him. I was so eager and anxious to see Anna that I was willing to brush him off without hesitation.

I arrived at the park. GPS sent me to the side entrance, unsure of where the yellow slide was. I had taken Sam to this park a few times prior, but could not remember ever seeing it. The park was minimally lit with some streetlights. I did recall the park was rather large, and I was hoping there was only one yellow slide. I took off to search for it. I didn't see it at the first playground I came across, only a red slide, so I continued to follow the sidewalk. I looked at my watch. 7:26 p.m. I had plenty of time to find it still. I could feel my heart racing, thumping hard against my chest as if it wanted to jump right out.

Calm down, I repeated to myself. I wanted to see Anna. Maybe she could help me understand some things, or explain something. I was desperate for her information at this point. She must have something important to tell me. But why was she acting so oddly about meeting me, leaving me notes, like she feared something or someone? It was then, mid-thought, that I spotted the yellow slide about thirty feet away. As I approached, I saw no sign of Anna, but I was 10 minutes early. I waited, patiently checking my watch. There were a few people in the park, a handful riding through on bikes, but no one I recognized from the flower shop or the grocery store. I watched a family pack up, a gentle father attempting to load two toddlers in the van as the kids screamed and cried and pointed toward the swings. I focused on the family, all the while experiencing jealousy of the normalcy the family displayed, just an ordinary family spending quality time at the park. I wondered what that felt like. *I would be a great mother*, I thought, *a normal mother, if I ever get the chance.* As I watched the family drive away in the white minivan, my phone rang, catching me off guard, hastily interrupting my visions of motherhood.

"Hello?" I said before even scanning the incoming phone number, assuming to hear Anna's voice on the other end.

"I am beginning to think you're not going to show up."

Everett, I thought. *Shit*. I began to apologize, now regretting ever picking up the line. "Something came up, I was rushed and didn't get the chance to call. I'm so sorry, Everett." I could hear my own genuineness about my voice. I did feel terrible about standing him up, but I was unavoidably preoccupied.

The sound of his voice pained me. He was disappointed. Story of my life, a disappointment. He warmly said he understood, and I hung up the phone. I knew he didn't understand. He was only being polite. I felt certain it was frustrating for him, especially after he shared something so personal and extreme just hours earlier. My phone once again began ringing, interrupting another thought. I looked down to see Sherry's number flicker across my screen. I right clicked it, noticing Anna was now 4 minutes late.

I spotted Anna walking on the path nearing closer to me. I had perched myself on the slide like a child, worried she wouldn't see me otherwise. She looked just as I remembered the last time I saw her at my mother's memorial. She was pretty, tall and thin, beautiful dark skin with petite features to complement her perfect frame. I could see she had aged, but in a lovely manner, soft, as she neared closer to me. As she approached, she said nothing, only drew me in for a hug so tightly that I had a hard time breathing. She looked around nervously before she took me by the hand and led me to the swings, still silent.

She stared at me, and I began to feel tense, waiting for her to speak first. She didn't speak at first; she started to cry, and subtle tears streamed down her face. She didn't try to wipe them away, she just let them fall. It felt like eternity before she did speak. "Quinn, I'm sorry. I let you down, I let your mother down." Her first words mimicked her note to me, an apology for not protecting me. As I processed her words, I first felt anger, angry that she must have known something, never stopping it, never looking back after she left. I wasn't in need of an apology. I bantered inside my head, hoping this was not what I had waited to hear. I needed any answers, anything about my mother she could give me. Maybe find closure of some sort. I feared I wouldn't get that.

"Before your mother left, she called me," she sniffled, finally wiping away her tears.

"What did she say?"

"She wanted me to look after you, to check in on you, to protect you."

"While she was gone?" I replied.

"She was afraid something was going to happen to her, she said in case she didn't return. You see, she told me she couldn't trust anyone, and that she knew I loved you and had grown close to you. I don't think she killed herself, Quinn. I think someone hurt her—well, killed her. Not someone, I mean— I think Brooks is responsible for it."

Anna went on to tell me that my mother was completely sober when they spoke, and that my mother was terrified. She told me that my mother was in a hole she couldn't dig herself out of. She was depressed and had nowhere to turn. She said Stella had thought about running away with me but didn't have the courage, and that Brooks had money and resources and that he would find us.

"Quinn, I was scared too. I turned my back. It was too much for me. I was young and terrified as well. I'm still scared. Brooks is still alive. I've seen him."

I felt my jaw lock up; I must have been gritting my teeth unknowingly while I listened. The jaw ache was now rushing my temple, giving me a relentless headache. I rubbed my temples, attempting to relieve the pressure so I could think straight.

"Anna, what do you mean Brooks is alive? I watched him die. I mean, I saw him stop breathing. Or I mean, I thought I did." My memory was now playing tricks on me. I was scanning my memories of that night, feeling fairly uncertain in the moment of what I recalled seeing. "THE PICTURES! There are pictures, Anna, my mother isn't the only person he hurt or killed, for that matter. I found something in the basement; Miles was there too. We found a box of pictures, awful pictures. Pictures of those girls they found dead in Beaufort. He did it, Anna."

The tears now rushed my face, making the headache even worse. They weren't subtle like Anna's, they were forceful, like a broken pipe. "I tried to tell Kent, they think I'm a crazy drug addict. And Miles—I don't even know what to say about him." I was now just vomiting out the mouth, my words trailing. Unsure if she could even make out what I was saying. I could tell by the look in her eyes she believed me. "This can't be, Anna, he can't be alive!"

"Listen to me carefully. He knows you're out of prison, where you live, and where you work. He has connections, important connections that trust him. He threatened me, tracked me down, and made me warn you—to keep you silent."

Chapter Now

"How can you be so calm about this?" I exclaimed, my hands trembling in disbelief as I awaited her response. "I saw him die, Anna. I know what I saw. There's no way he's alive. This is insane." Anna sighed deeply, her expression weighted with concern. "Quinn, I understand why you're scared and confused. But you have to listen to me. Brooks . . . he's alive. I've seen him, talked to him."

My heart skipped a beat. "No, Anna, you must be mistaken," I protested, my voice wavering. "It's impossible. He can't be alive." Anna stayed in the swing, calmly looking down as she kicked around the rubber mulch nervously. I assume she was at a loss for words. She finally looked back up at me and stood from the swing; she had begun to shed tears again. She took my cheeks into her hands, "Quinn, please. He will hurt you, maybe even . . ." She paused before saying it. "Kill you. Just tell me you'll keep quiet, and this will go away."

I angrily pulled my face from her hands. "He murdered my mother! And now you're telling me he's alive? He's a monster who needs to pay for what he has done! He's manipulating you and now threatening me, and you expect me to just sit here silently, Anna?" I paused to inhale deeply, exhaling slowly as

Helen had taught me during our time locked up. Speaking again, my tone shifted. "He sent you here because he thinks I'll believe you, doesn't he? Thinks I'll trust you and give him what he wants. Well, I can't, Anna. If I had proof, those pictures, I would turn him in. I would take him down."

Anna kept her composure, although she was still quietly crying. "I am staying with a friend near Beaufort. I'm scared, Quinn. I think someone has been following me. I just wanted you to know about your mother, and I was told to warn you. I'm sorry. I should go."

I could feel a hint of remorse come over me, empathizing with Anna, being thrown into such a dreadful situation.

"Anna, I shouldn't have yelled at you. Please come and stay a night with me. I don't want to be alone tonight." And I didn't. I didn't want to be alone. I knew tonight I would relapse if I were alone. I needed a distraction, and I still had more questions for Anna.

I could tell she didn't want to, and after a brief pause, she looked me in the eyes and reached for my hand. She knew I needed her tonight, and that was all she could do for me to help me.

On the walk to my car, I thought about Sherry. I always thought about Sherry when I felt weak or compromised. I sent her a text knowing she would be wondering why I didn't make it tonight. *I'm okay Sherry, just a big day at work and I'm exhausted. Will catch up soon I promise.*

Anna followed me back to my apartment. I sensed her apprehension while we made our way up to my door. I could hear Sam pawing at the door as I jiggled the key to unlock it, happily awaiting my arrival.

"Anna, please make yourself a glass of water or tea. Just look in the fridge and get what you want. I need to run him downstairs, but I'll be back in five."

I grabbed Sam's leash and took off downstairs to our area, my big tree still standing there out front protecting me most days from the blazing sun or rain as I hover beneath it while Sam takes his time doing his business. Once again, I took the sight in, bringing some momentary peace to me. Not rushing over to it, knowing I didn't want to leave Anna waiting long.

When I returned upstairs, Anna had made a glass of water and was sitting on the couch, looking lost and still concerned.

I shut the door and let Sam off his leash. "He's a good guard dog. I mean, he won't bite or attack, but he will alert me," I said, trying to bring her some comfort. I was glad she was there; it was easier to fight the feeling of going out to buy myself a drink or whatever else I could get my hands on.

"Anna, what did Brooks do to you?" I asked, my voice steady but filled with concern as we sat across from each other on the couch.

Anna hesitated, her gaze dropping to her hands clasped tightly in her lap. "It's . . . hard to talk about," she admitted quietly, her voice tinged with pain. "He . . . he hurt me, Quinn. Physically. And emotionally."

My heart sank, anger rising within me. "I'm so sorry, Anna," I murmured, knowing the exact pain she spoke of.

She gave a sad smile, appreciating my concern. "Thanks, Quinn. It's something I've tried to bury deep down, but he's never really gone away, has he?"

"No," I said firmly. "He hasn't. He's been terrorizing us both, in different ways."

Anna nodded, her expression turning somber. "After what he did, I couldn't keep playing the violin. It just . . . reminded me of better times before he came into my life. We were both so talented," she said softly, making me recall how she used to light up whenever she played for me "It's not fair what he took from us. And now he sends me money," Anna continued bitterly, shaking her head. "As if that makes up for everything. It's like he's trying to buy my silence, to keep me under his control."

"He's trying to keep us both quiet," I replied, my voice hardening. "But we can't let him win, Anna. We have to find a way to stop him."

Anna met my gaze, determination flickering in her eyes. "You're right, Quinn. We can't let him keep doing this to us. We have to find a way to fight back."

"We will," I affirmed, reaching for her hand across the couch. "Together."

Sherry sent me a text message during my chat with Anna, *I would like to see you soon. I know you're busy but make time or I'll show up.* I knew she would. I will call her tomorrow and settle her down and agree to meet. She hated it when I missed meetings, knowing how delicate I once was. I didn't feel delicate in this turmoil. I wanted justice and was willing to do anything to expose Brooks. I needed to get Miles on board, though.

"People think he is dead, Anna. I mean, he really covered his tracks. You are certain? I mean, you said you have seen him, right?" I asked cautiously.

"Not everyone thinks he is dead, some people know he is still alive, in 'witness protection,'" she said sarcastically, using air quotations as she said those words. "What a joke. He really is a con artist, playing the victim."

"Witness protection? Makes sense, he has connections," I said.

That was the first inkling of bravery or mockery I had witnessed from Anna since meeting up with her. The sound of her voice was stark when she told me about the witness protection scam. I was hopeful that our conversations were stirring up some emotional trauma that she would soon release by helping me figure out how to get revenge or justice. I would settle for either.

I managed to talk Anna into staying with me for a few days and going to pay Miles a visit the following day. Maybe united we could convince him to help us.

Chapter Now

THE NEXT MORNING, I familiarized Anna with my apartment, showing her where I kept the towels and such. She planned on making a quick trip to the supermarket to grab a toothbrush but then hanging out with Sam until I was able to return home from the flower shop.

During my drive to work, I practiced my apology out loud to Everett for the night before. I was sincere, but that social awkwardness would show its ugly face and I would make a mess of it. So, I decided practicing out loud would help. He would believe me; after all, I had the bags under my eyes to prove it. I looked exhausted, and I was, but somehow a jolt of adrenaline from Anna's arrival was keeping me going strong and had propelled me into superwoman. I looked more tired on the outside than I felt on the inside.

I thought about Miles during my car ride too, the fact that he hadn't even called after the night we had spent together. It didn't matter, I didn't matter. *I should be used to this*, I thought, *but onto bigger fish*, I told myself. *I deal with him soon enough; I'll convince him to do the right thing.*

Everett had beat me to work. He had ridden his bike as he often did, and it was chained in front of the store. I walked in to find a warm cup of coffee in a paper cup with my name on it sitting on the ledge of my worktable. He had his head down, pretending to be working as I clutched the cup and took a sip. I looked over at him, staring a hole through him until he looked up at me.

"Thank you for the coffee, Everett," I said with a shy, forgiving grin draped across my face. I was testing the waters, seeing if he would bite at my attempt to make up.

He stared at me without saying thank you. "You look like you had a long night," he said, his tone holding sarcasm, clearly taking my bait. He enjoyed being sarcastically insensitive at times, as if it were a game between us. Knowing I liked to awkwardly laugh things off, his comments always provided the perfect opportunity.

I shot back with a smirk, "Oh, thanks for pointing that out, Captain Obvious. Did you stay up all night thinking of that one?"

Everett grinned, unfazed by my comeback. "Nah, just keeping it fresh for you. Someone's gotta keep you on your toes around here."

I rolled my eyes, "I don't know what I'd do without your charming sarcasm in my life."

He chuckled softly, a hint of flirtation in his voice. "Probably be bored out of your mind. Admit it, you love it."

"Maybe just a little," I admitted, glancing around the shop. "But you're lucky I'm in a forgiving mood today."

"Oh, I'm counting my blessings," Everett replied with mock seriousness, flashing me a lopsided grin.

I couldn't help but smile back. Despite the teasing banter, there was an undeniable warmth between us that made the day a little more bearable.

He then diverted his gaze back to his arrangement, adjusting the spray with such seriousness. I had gleaned insight into his behavior and personality, understanding his way of lightening the mood to ease my discomfort. It was as if he was pretending this morning was like any other, using his snide remarks to secretly convey that he had already forgiven me.

By lunch, I was growing restless. I had sent Anna a message to be sure she was making herself at home. She was. I was being over-worrisome. I had sent Sherry a message promising to meet for coffee this weekend, and she accepted my word. Although my mind was bogged down with random thoughts, my main concern was Brooks at that point. Even though I was still pissed at Miles, I was still planning on trying to get him on board with helping me and Anna. Why? Why, if he knew his dad was alive, would he be worried about telling the truth? I mean, he obviously wasn't guilty of anything; he didn't kill him. I couldn't get my mind to process the reason he was protecting this awful monster. I planned on finding out.

I left work in a hurry, not even telling Everett goodbye. I felt guilty by the time I reached my car, so I sent him a text. *Have a great night, sorry for rushing out. Thanks for understanding and forgiving me. Lots going on with me.*

He left me on "read." I was certain he was done with me; I wasn't able to give him much of me, and he was dealing with his own matters. I didn't blame him. He was better off.

When I arrived home, Anna was sitting at the kitchen table with her eyes fixed on her phone, barely making eye contact with me as I walked in.

"What's wrong, Anna?" I immediately asked.

"Nothing," she replied again, not making eye contact. I could tell that wasn't the case. She was obviously shaken up. I took a seat at the table with her.

"Anna, talk to me. Please. What's happened?"

"Today, there was a knock on your door. I didn't answer, but later I opened the door to find this." She handed me a white, folded piece of paper. I began to unfold the paper, my hands visibly shaking. I didn't feel scared, but most definitely I was nervous, apprehensive about what I was unfolding.

The note was nicely written in cursive, almost appearing as if a woman had written it, with black ink displayed neatly across the lines. The letter read, *Run. Do not look back. Nothing is as it seems. They will do anything to keep their secret.*

"Nothing is as it seems," I muttered to myself, my thoughts racing. "What does this mean? Who are 'they'?" Anna remained seated, her gaze fixed on the letter in a deafening silence. Adrenaline and anger surged through me in equal measure, a familiar pairing of emotions lately.

"Get up, Anna," I urged firmly, reaching out to gently nudge her arm, prompting her to rise from the table. Instead, she continued to stare at me, as if contemplating escape from this ordeal. She was an innocent dragged into a tragedy, but I refused to shoulder the blame alone.

"Anna!" I raised my voice, more insistent this time. "Get up," I commanded.

"Quinn," Anna finally spoke, her voice barely above a whisper, "I don't know if I can do this."

I turned to face her, seeing the fear and uncertainty etched on her face. "You have to," I replied firmly. "We need to confront this together."

She hesitated, her eyes darting between me and the letter in her hand. "I'm scared, Quinn," Anna admitted, her voice trembling slightly. "What if he comes after us?"

"We won't let him," I reassured her, though doubt gnawed at my own resolve. "Miles needs to know what's going on. We can't do this alone."

Anna nodded slowly, taking a deep breath to steady herself. "Okay," she said finally, her voice steadier now. "Let's go."

Chapter **Now**

WE ARRIVED AT the ER, my adrenaline still coursing through me. I bypassed the check-in station and slipped through the double doors just as they opened for an elderly couple exiting to the waiting room. Gripping Anna's hand, I hurried forward, keeping my gaze straight ahead and silently praying that the triage nurse was preoccupied—luckily, she was.

The ER bustled with activity; patients lined the hallways on stretchers, but nothing appeared immediately urgent. There were no screams or urgent commotions, just enough busyness to keep the staff occupied and oblivious to our stealthy entry.

"That nurse, the redhead," I whispered to Anna, pointing discreetly at the nurse stationed at the desk. "She knows me."

I made my way to her. "Hi," I said as I leaned over the counter to grab her attention. She looked up from her computer in a non-enthusiastic manner.

"Can I help you?" she asked, sounding extremely insincere with her question, all while perching one eyebrow to let me know I was a nuisance and undoubtedly had interrupted her. She sat there with her fingers still resting on her keyboard, waiting for me to answer making intense eye contact.

"Well, um—do you remember me? I was with Dr. Brooks, we met once."

"So?" Her eyes did roll this time.

I could tell she was becoming bothered by my presence. "Is he here tonight?" I asked, ignoring her attitude.

"Nope," she said breaking eye contact and beginning to type again as if I weren't still standing there. I looked at Anna, waiting for her to miraculously come up with our next move.

The redheaded nurse stopped typing, looking up at me once again. Her head cocked over to the side before she spoke, "Yeah, he did the same thing to me. Used ya and moved on. He's not here, but I can tell you where he is—probably downtown at The Chophouse eating dinner with his wife." She rolled her eyes once again before returning to her computer. I looked at Anna with a surprised look upon my face. I could feel my cheeks burning.

"His wife?" I whispered silently towards Anna.

"Yeah, sweetheart, his wife. He's married. Surprise. Guess he left that part out." She was still typing as I stood there stunned. She displayed no emotion or attention to me after her revelation.

A physician emerged from out of nowhere, seemingly in a hurry. "Let's move, we have a significant fall with a head laceration, move someone out of seven." He was clearly speaking to the red headed nurse. There was no goodbye or good luck. In fact, there was no acknowledgment from the nurse at all before she rose from her chair and disappeared down the hallway.

"What the hell?" I mouthed out loud, not necessarily to Anna, but to myself. Anna just stood there, nothing emerging from her mouth. She looked like a lost puppy separated from the litter, wondering where to go next.

I grabbed her hand once again and led the way to the

parking lot and back to the car. We sat in silence for what felt like twenty minutes.

I had my hands on the steering wheel, never actually starting the car. I was staring ahead at nothing, only replaying that night with Miles in my head.

"He's married, Anna. He never mentioned a wife. I mean he took me to dinner. He SLEPT with me," I said crossly. I could feel my hands throbbing. I was grasping the steering wheel forcefully, cutting off the circulation, I supposed.

Anna didn't respond. She was of no help in the matter. She sat there quietly, lost in her own thoughts.

I started the car. "Anna, pull up directions to The Chophouse. Let's go," I demanded in a harsh tone.

She did as she was instructed, and we arrived at the restaurant twenty minutes later, once again to find ourselves sitting silently in the car. I wasn't sure what on earth I wanted to even say at this point. I needed some advice on the whole Brooks situation, but I also wanted to confront him about his infidelity with me, and his omittance about having a wife. He was a fraud. *Explains why he never called,* I thought.

I glanced at my watch. It was getting late. "He could be gone by now," I said to Anna. She was still hushed, having nothing to add.

I barged into The Chophouse bypassing the hostess. The place was nice, elegant lighting hovering the tables. It was exactly what I pictured; a fancy venue where the rich and exclusive would gather to feed their mouths and discuss the stock market. I wasn't dressed for the occasion, and looking down at myself, I felt a bit out of place, but nonetheless I continued my search for Miles, passing table after table. Several people stared as I hurried by, and I could feel the hostess behind me, gaining on me. Anna was walking directly behind me, mimicking my every step. I spotted him in the back sitting across from a blonde woman that seemed to be gazing at him from her seat.

"Ma'am." The hostess touched my shoulder, inviting me to stop, and I did. I looked at her, and her eyes were wide, like she could tell I was upset. "Can I help you?" she asked uncertainly. "No, thank you. I have found who I was looking for." I turned and looked towards the back at Miles. He had still not noticed me. The girl was clutching a menu in her hand, unsure if she were going to ask me to leave or let me go ahead. I didn't give her the opportunity to ask me to leave. I continued towards the back, Anna followed.

My presence caught Miles off guard. He instantly stood from his seat, his face turning pale as if the blood were draining rapidly from it.

"Quinn," he said, shocked, immediately looking over at the blonde.

I drew my attention to her as well, sticking out my hand hostilely towards her. "Hello there, you must be Mrs. Barlow. So very lovely to meet you," I said with sarcasm rolling off my tongue.

The blonde never reached out for my hand, she only glanced back over at Miles with red cheeks and a look of confusion spewed across her face. Miles placed his hand on my back, gesturing for me to move from the table. "Let's go outside, Quinn."

I maneuvered my way from his hand. "No, I think we will join you two. Anna?" I looked over at Anna, only she wasn't there.

Miles's horrified stare amplified, "Quinn, I think we should continue this outside." This time he whispered, trying not to draw any more attention to our table. I was finding satisfaction in his squirming, his embarrassment.

Miles was becoming flustered; his face still pale but his

cheeks blushed, and the surrounding tables began to whisper and gawk. "Honey, I'm sorry, she's ill. She is a patient of mine. Please just grab your purse and things and I'll meet you at the car."

"A goddamn patient, Miles?!" This time I yelled; I could feel my hands waving in the air from infuriation.

The blonde was on her feet now, gathering her belongings from the table, hastily slipping on her shawl.

A gentleman wearing a white shirt with a black vest appeared out of nowhere. "Dr. Barlow, is there a problem?" His eyes were locked on me, judging my being. I assumed he was the manager coming to rescue Miles from the insane patient they let slip through the gaudy doors.

I glanced over at his wife, edging closer as she adjusted her wrap over her shoulder. "I'm not a patient! Do you sleep with all your patients, Miles?" I shouted, locking eyes with him. Then I turned to his wife. "I'm his stepsister. It's complicated, but I really need to talk to him. It's urgent." Scanning the room for Anna; I called out louder, "Anna! Anna!" I needed her help to persuade him to listen to us.

Miles was now standing between me and his wife; more waiters and staff had gathered. I felt as if I were a cow about to be corralled through the shoot.

"Quinn, who are you talking to?" He had now taken my arm and began pulling me towards the front. I yanked my arm away from him briskly. "What do you mean who am I talking to?" His question threw me for a loop.

"Anna?" he questioned.

I stopped, still scanning my view for Anna, I couldn't find her. "She was just here." She had disappeared from sight. "Anna, Miles, Anna. You know Anna, she was just right here. She must be out front."

I began walking out front with a fleet of staff following

closely behind me. Miles was at the end, coddling his wife in his arms, acting as if I had just assaulted her.

I swung the door open, hoping to find Anna standing on the sidewalk in front of the restaurant. The staff stopped at the front, deciding not to follow me out. I could see Miles inside the doors, on his cell phone, seemingly having an intense conversation. His blonde wife was closely by his side, with subtle tears streaming down her flushed cheeks.

I started walking to the car. "Anna!" I yelled out, hoping to find her lurking in the parking lot waiting for me. "Anna?" I called out again. The car was empty.

Miles was now making his way towards me in the parking lot. His walk was heavy, reminding me of Brooks, with his dark eyes and serious expression.

"Miles, listen, Anna came to help me, we need your help. She has a note. I mean, Brooks is threatening us. Just let me find her. She can explain. He sent her to warn me." I was babbling and I knew it.

Miles was shaking his head. "Stop, Quinn. Stop." I went silent, waiting for him to say more. "Anna, your tutor Anna from long ago? Is this who you were talking to in the restaurant?"

"YES! Brooks sent her to warn me, to intimidate me. He's still playing his sick games, can't you see it, Miles!" I was frantic, still searching for any sign of Anna.

"Quinn, Anna was found in Albergotti Creek. She's dead. And dad, Quinn—he's gone too."

Chapter Now

I WOKE TO A ray of sun peeking through a window covered with black steel bars. I rubbed my eyes, wondering if I were imagining the scene. The room was bare, cement walls and floors, and nothing but a bed and a mattress occupied the room. I frantically rose from the bed, feeling groggy, with a headache pounding my right temple. This familiar feeling rushed my body. It felt like as if I had been on a week binger and I was coming out of it. *I didn't slip, I know I didn't slip. Where am I? Did I go to jail?*

I got up out of the bed, instinctually searching for my cell, knowing I would not find it. I flipped the mattress off the bed. The door opened. "Quinn, are you okay, dear? Let me help you." I turned to see a woman dressed in white scrubs, early 40s, soft voice, approaching me.

"Where the fuck am I?" I asked, not so politely. The throbbing sensation hit me as I did so. My head ached so intensely.

She kneeled beside the bed, lifting the mattress back onto the frame. "Sit down," she said as she patted the bed, inviting me to sit. She took a seat first. I was hesitant, but I sat across from her on the other side waiting for an explanation. "You are at the Statesboro Mental health facility. You have been legally admitted for treatment." Her relaxed demeanor helped my panic level not escalate off the charts. Her voice was gentle and calming.

I took a deep breath, trying to recall in my head what had happened. The headache was so powerful I was having a hard time thinking straight. The last thing I could remember was Miles. He was standing there telling me that Anna was dead. I massaged my temple, attempting to ease the throbbing pressure.

"That's normal, the headache you have. You were given an antipsychotic drug last night to help you calm down. I would be glad to get you something to ease the ache. When I return, I will take your blood pressure and pulse. Then we can talk more about why you are here."

I nodded my head, unable to contest due to the relentless pain in my head and groggy fog lingering over my body.

The nurse returned fairly quickly with a small cupful of medication. She handed the meds to me along with a plastic cup filled with water.

"What is all this?" I asked before gulping down the water. I was thirsty, my mouth dry and sticky, like I had swallowed a handful of cotton balls the night before.

"Those are medications the doctor has prescribed, to help you feel better."

"What doctor? I haven't seen a doctor. I feel fine, other than this headache," I replied.

"Take the medication, and we can talk about why you are here." She nudged the cupful of medicine towards my mouth.

I followed her instructions, though I protested; the pain was so severe I didn't have the energy to argue. "Can I have my phone?" I asked the nurse as I handed her back the empty cup.

"Who would you like to call?" she calmly asked.

"How did I get here?" I inquired once again.

She was placing the blood pressure cuff around my arm, ignoring the question momentarily.

"Please tell me," I begged quietly.

She removed the cuff, still sitting beside me, she answered, "You were hallucinating. Hallucinations are very serious and require treatment. You have a history of mental illness and drug use, so your doctor has decided its best that you be monitored properly."

"My doctor?" I asked. "Who? Who is my doctor?"

"Dr. Barlow. He has admitted you; however, you are now under the care of Dr. Sara Newsome, whom you will be meeting later today."

I could feel my eyes becoming heavy, my thoughts drifting away. I suddenly felt the need to lie down. *What did they give me . . .*

Chapter Now

I T WAS DARK, with no sunshine filtering through the windows protected by black bars. The headache had subsided, though I still felt a bit drowsy. I had hoped to wake up in my own bed, wishing this was all just a nightmare. Yet, here I was, still surrounded by bare cement walls. I couldn't decide which was worse: facing the reality of Miles and his blonde wife, or entertaining the fantasy spun by Anna about Brooks being alive. I wasn't entirely convinced Anna was dead. Claudia claimed to have seen her, but was it really her? Was someone trying to drive me insane, or was I losing my mind on my own? The thought paralyzed me as I attempted to make my way to the door. Could I have been hallucinating? Was I on the brink of a certified mental breakdown? I needed to talk to someone. Gripping the doorknob, I turned it, fully expecting it to be locked. To my surprise, it opened. I cautiously peered out into the hallway, where several figures in white scrubs were gathered around the nurse's station.

"Excuse me," I said stepping out into the hallway. "Can I see my doctor, please?"

"Hi, there." I was greeted by the same nurse that had given me the medicine earlier. She was courteous, nodding her head in response to my question. "Of course, she has been waiting for you to wake. I'll let her know you are awake now. Just wait in your room. May I bring you some water?"

"Please, that would be great. But can I use the phone? Or have my phone back?" As the words exited my mouth it felt dry, my tongue sticking to my teeth and the roof of my mouth. I desperately needed the water.

The nurse came closer and gently patted my arm in a subtle attempt to comfort me, "Let's talk to the doctor first, then maybe we can let you use the phone. We have let your emergency contact know you're here, and she should be here around 6 during visiting hours to see you. I'll grab you some water."

As she turned around, I instinctively grabbed her arm, surprised at her previous announcement. "Wait, who did you let know?" It had surprised me; I mean, I had no emergency contact. After a brief pause, I let her arm go. "I have no family." Wow. Hearing myself say that out loud was like a gut punch. I sounded pathetic. It stirred up emotions that I had buried, or so I had thought. Not one person had come to visit me in jail. I fought back a stream of tears that I could feel surging my eyes, but before they could begin falling, she answered me.

"Sherry Fitz. She was listed as your emergency contact in your phone, she said she was coming today." She looked down at her arm momentarily before walking away to grab my water and the doctor.

Sherry, thank goodness. Her name brought relief to my being. I had a lot of explaining to do.

I waited impatiently for the doctor, pacing the cold floors. I had on a gown, unsure of how it got there, and my feet heavy as I strode from one corner of the room to the other. The bottoms of my feet were black, and all I could think about was how thirsty I felt, like I could drink a lake. I needed to get out of here. I decided then I wouldn't take another medication they tried to give me. I didn't even really know how long I had been here, a day or a week. My memory was hazy, and I recalled the evening with Miles, but beyond that I drew a blank. The doctor arrived, and she was tall and pretty. Younger than I expected. "Hi, Miss Barlow, take a seat," she said as the nurse followed behind, pushing in a chair behind her. The nurse left the chair behind Dr. Newsome, and after handing me a plastic cup full of water, she exited the room, closing the door behind her.

I set the cup beside the bed and sat down, intensely focused on the upcoming conversation that was about to follow. I heard myself sigh aloud as I did. "I'm sorry, please just call me Quinn." I fidgeted around the mattress before settling. "I just . . . I'm not sure why I am here. I don't mean to be rude."

"No need to apologize. My name is Dr. Sara Newsome. You were brought here by Dr. Miles Barlow, and your brother Kent Barlow, after an intense mental break that included visual and auditory hallucinations. They are concerned regarding your past use of drugs, worried you may harm yourself, or others."

I interrupted her and stood to my feet. "A mental breakdown!" I laughed sarcastically and forcefully. "I am not using, and Anna, well—she certainly felt real to me! She even came to my work. She wrote me notes. Call Claudia, she saw her." I could feel my hands waving in the air as I summoned her to call Claudia.

Dr. Newsome opened a manila folder, it held what looked like a clipping of a newspaper that had been printed off. "Your brother Kent gave this to me. It's an article from the paper in Beaufort. Would you like to take a look?" She stood from her chair, approaching me, holding out the paper for me to take.

I grabbed the paper from her hand and started to read. Anna's name was highlighted in yellow. Warm tears welled up in my eyes involuntarily. Had I imagined her? My mouth suddenly felt intensely dry once again. I sat on the bed, reaching for my water and chugging it down completely, never taking my eyes off the paper. I rubbed my eyes, but the clipping still showed the same information. "It appears that this tragic situation has triggered these hallucinations. Hallucinations can often accompany underlying mental conditions, particularly given your family history. Your brothers provided me with a detailed account of your mother's illness and her suicide. Quinn, regarding your beliefs about your stepfather, it seems these delusions may also stem from a mental health disorder. It appears you've become disconnected from reality," she continued.

"Bullshit!" I screamed. I found myself pacing once again. *Okay, Quinn, don't make yourself appear crazy. Calm down, breathe in and out, in and out.*

"It's likely that your transition from prison back into society, coupled with the tragic events in your hometown, has heightened your mental health instability. I believe the news of Anna's body being found triggered this." Her jargon wasn't convincing me that I'd had a total psychological collapse, but I needed her on my side. Although something told me that I was going to be here for awhile, if Miles had anything to do with it.

"What about Brooks, my stepfather? Is he dead or not? Anna insisted he's alive. And my mother wasn't sick; she was an alcoholic, that's the truth. She suffered abuse from my stepfather, just as I did!" My body quivered with emotion; I struggled to maintain composure and seem collected, but beneath the surface, anger simmered like a volcano ready to erupt. I paced incessantly, unable to remain still.

"Tell me about the abuse, Quinn," she responded softly, appearing sincerely concerned.

"How long do you have? You won't believe what I am about to tell you."

Chapter Now

"THANK YOU FOR picking me up, Sherry. You just don't know how much your support over the last few months has meant to me," I said as I finished bagging up the few personal belongings that I did have with me.

"Now, don't be upset, but Sam has gained a few pounds. Turns out he likes to eat what I eat, and his puppy dog eyes—it was hard to say no," she said as her forehead puckered, and her mouth flashed a mischievous smile. She and Sam had bonded. She would visit each week, sharing with me Sam's doings from the week prior: what couch corner he had gnawed on or which neighbors' dogs he had become friends with. I was feeling guilty that I was about to take her new best friend from her after all she had done for me.

"I sure have missed him. You think he missed me?" I asked, almost dreading her response. I knew Sherry had taken good care of him, probably spoiling him even more than I ever had. *Why would he want to come home with me?* I thought.

She gave a slight smirk, saying, "Yeah, he missed ya, sweetie," as she patted me on the back.

"Let's get out of here before they change their mind," I laughed, heading towards the door. Glancing around one last time at the cement walls and floors, it felt like a bittersweet departure. Here, between these walls, I had found Dr. Newsome, courage, and strength. These cement floors supported me as I told my story. Someone had listened, believed, and fought for me, but I knew it was just the beginning.

I arrived at home to a door decorated with streamers. "What in the world, Sherry," I said, turning around to give her an uncertain smile. "You know I was just released from a loony bin? I mean, I guess that's worth celebrating." My own statement made me laugh quietly. I was secretly feeling delighted, grateful that she cared so much about me, and that she had not deserted me.

I could hear Sam, once again anticipating my arrival, or someone's arrival. I wondered briefly if he thought that I had abandoned him never to return. My hand was shaking as I unlocked the door from excitement, anxious to be reunited with him, and my bed. I had missed my bed terribly.

"SURPRISE!" I opened the door to see Everett and Claudia standing right there in my kitchen with their hands up in the air as if they were cheering on a birthday girl. Their faces presented genuine smiles, and before I knew it, Claudia had wrapped her arms firmly around me for an uncomfortable amount of time. I managed to shimmy away from her grip.

"Sam!" He had jumped on me, pressing his paws into my abdomen and licking at my arms, begging for my attention.

"See, I told you he missed you," Sherry bellowed. Everyone was standing around me. Still feeling embarrassed, I knelt down to pet Sam's head.

"We all missed you, Quinn," Everett softly added. "Glad you're home." He slowly walked over to me and gently pulled me off the ground and into a hug. It felt weird and I made it worse with my awkwardness. My hands wouldn't manage to hug him back, they gawkily hung while he embraced me in his chest. "I knew you would hate this," he whispered sneakily in my ear as he released me from his mild hold.

"Thank you," I said as I made eye contact with Everett while he pulled away. He gave me a wink before turning around to grab something from my countertop. "Nonalcoholic wine, anyone?" he said as he held up a bottle of some sort of imitation wine.

My face burned as red as a stop sign, and my shoulders slumped in shame. It took some nerve to voice my skepticism about the party, but finally, I blurted out, "Thank you all, but what exactly are we celebrating? I just got released from a psych ward; it's not my birthday!" I finished with a nervous laugh.

Claudia immediately made her way to me and placed her hand on my cheek. "Honey, this is a celebration of you. We love you and support you. We're glad you are home and healthy. That's what we are celebrating. It's what friends and family do."

I was clenching my bottom lip between my teeth and fighting back the happy tears. *Family,* I thought. *Wow.* I was speechless, and I let the happy tears plunge down my face without care, releasing the clench on my mouth. Claudia wrapped me up once again, and this time I didn't pull away and I didn't feel embarrassed: I felt loved.

Everett interrupted the moment, "Okay, okay, enough of this nonsense. Let's have some cake and you can tell us stories about the crazy people you made friends with." He was smirking as usual as he began to dig through my cabinets in search of glasses for our make-do wine.

"I agree," Sherry interjected as she joined Everett in search of utensils to cut the cake and serve the pretend wine. Sherry looked over at me as I still stood there taking it all in. "Quinn, Claudia and I have become quite good friends, almost as good

as me and Sam. I'm not sure I'm ready to return either one!"
she said as she laughed.

I looked over at Claudia, fearful she now knew the truth
about me, that I was an addict who lied to her. "Claudia, I'm
sorry. I . . ." I paused.

"Darling, there's no need to apologize. Life is unpredictable,
and sometimes things happen beyond our control. I've learned
that over the years. It's time to focus on doing what's right and
moving forward. We're here for you now—you're not alone."
Those words, that moment, took my breath right from my
lungs. I sighed, of relief, nothing else. I knew she meant every
word.

"Let's have cake," I said as I wiped away the remainder of the
tears that amassed my cheeks. I wanted to relish in this moment
with my new family.

Chapter Now

I REFLECTED ON THE evening as I sat with Sam and my new family, discussing what lie ahead for me. The diagnosis of psychosis had initially been hard to accept, but with my current situation at home and feeling somewhat stable, I was starting to come around to Dr. Newsome's assessment, but I wasn't entirely convinced. As for Miles, I held conflicting thoughts; I wanted to forgive him, but I planned on keeping my guard up. After all, Dr. Newsome did convince me that Anna was a hallucination.

My company stayed for hours, laughing as if nothing had ever happened. Everett shared his plans about opening an art studio, which filled me with pride. His return to painting sparked hope for my own future.

"Well, I think I better head home, I have a long drive." Sherry's words carried a weight as she rose from the couch, attention turning to bid farewell to Sam rather than me.

"I'm sure he will miss you too, you know," I said as I grabbed for her hand and gently gave it a squeeze. She patted him one last time, bent over to give me a kiss on the forehead, then rushed out the door. I thought she might cry, but she disappeared before she could.

Claudia had made her way to the kitchen to tidy up before leaving. "Well, Quinn, you still have a job if you are up for it. George is having his rotator cuff worked on. Getting old isn't for the weak, I will tell you that much. So, with Everett gone, I could use the help. Think about it, sweetie," she said before grabbing her purse. I pushed Sam down from my lap and followed her to the kitchen.

"Yeah, I think I'd like that. Dr. Newsome said that would be a great idea for me. I have a few appointments this next week, but I'll call you after that. And thank you, for everything." I gave her one last hug before she scurried out.

Everett approached me as we were left alone. "Now we can really talk," he said, attempting to lighten the mood with a laugh.

"About the loony bin?" I said. "I have plenty of stories!" I replied with an awkward laugh, unaware of his mood—was he serious or making light as usual?

He uncrossed his arms, and his mouth opened to speak, but he paused as if collecting his thoughts. His posture tightened, taking a couple of steps closer before stopping.

"Quinn, I mean really talk. I know I give you a hard time and tease you a lot, but you can talk to me." He paused again. "Are you really okay?" he asked sincerely. "A lot has happened to you."

"For the first time in a long time, I can tell you the truth. I'm okay. If anything, I'm embarrassed. Embarrassed that I had no idea I was sick, I had no idea I was delusional. For years, Everett. I'm humiliated." I left him standing near the kitchen, dumping myself onto the couch face-first like a child.

He followed, sitting on the couch across from me, waiting for me to sit upright like an adult, not rushing me, letting me have my moment of mortifying reality. He joined me, letting me fall asleep with my head in his lap.

Chapter Now

I WOKE IN MY bed, with Sam bundled in the covers next to me. I couldn't remember getting there, but I was sure it was the excitement and the exhaustion of the prior day. The sunshine beamed through the curtains, bringing warmth to my being. No black bars decorated the beams, which felt foreign only momentarily.

Everett. I jumped up from the bed to see if he had stayed. I couldn't remember him leaving. I wondered if I would find him asleep on my couch, but I didn't. He was nowhere to be found, which was actually a relief. I wanted to rediscover my space alone, or with Sam, anyways.

Everything was as I left it, clean and tidy. Someone, I assumed Claudia, had kept my plants alive while I was gone. I only had a few, ones she hadn't been able to sell and just plain wanted them to have a home. The feeling was odd, standing there in my own living room, reconnecting with my area, my things; it was almost reflective, surreal. For a moment I felt sorry for myself, so young, such tragedies I had witnessed, but I quickly reminded myself that some things were out of my control. I grabbed Sam's leash and my cell phone, deciding it was time to power the phone back on and rejoin civilization for the second time in my life.

I turned on the phone while I released Sam to do his business. I looked up to see him dragging along his leash, making his way to my tree to use it as a commode. I sat on the bench and stared at the phone that displayed 17 voicemail alerts. Most of them I knew would be hagglers, attempting to sell me something like a home warranty or such, but remarkably, 2 were from Kent. None from Miles. What a surprise. Not a visit from either one during my three-month retreat. Dr. Newsome had revealed that she was keeping in contact with both, but neither bothered to visit me or even call. I had discouraged Claudia and Everett from coming; I didn't feel comfortable with them seeing me there, in that place and in that circumstance. Sherry would deliver hellos, and sometimes Claudia and Everett would call and check in on me, always keeping the conversations light and brief.

I wasn't ready to listen to Kent's voicemails yet. Dr. Newsome had convinced me that Anna was a hallucination, and that Brooks was not able to hurt me anymore, but I was still getting used to the idea.

"Sam! Come here," I called out, clapping my hands to get his attention. He trotted over, and I stooped down to scratch behind his ears. "Let's go, Sam. We've got some catching up to do." I powered on my phone to make a few calls, including one to schedule an appointment with my new psychiatrist, a condition of my release. Despite feeling it was a waste of time, I played along, trying to keep Dr. Newsome's trust. Nonetheless, I remained perplexed. Why was Miles so determined to portray me as irrational? Why was he unwilling to help me reveal the truth about who his father really was? I was baffled because Brooks's death was an accident; he was protecting me. Deep down, I knew Miles had orchestrated the letter to Claudia. She wasn't delusional; that much was clear.

Chapter **Now**

S AM AND I settled in at home as best I could. I found myself sitting on the couch, half-expecting the nurse in white to appear and offer me my little blue pill. I had taken the pills. If I hadn't, I would still be surrounded by grey walls and dirty concrete floors. The appointment with my new psychiatrist was scheduled for the following day, a condition of my release that I couldn't avoid. Seated with Sam at my feet, a touch of discouragement weighed on me. I continued grappling with distinguishing reality from imagination. Anna's presence seemed incredibly real, whether standing before me or seated in my kitchen. Accepting that it was all fabrication, a trick my mind concocted, was challenging. Fatigued from the ongoing turmoil, I was nearing acceptance of the uncertainty. My phone rang, knocking me out of my reflections.

"Hello," I answered.

"Good morning, Quinn. I hope you rested well."

"Everett. I did, for the most part. Thank you, for . . . well, just being there last night."

"No problem. I mean, it's not every day a friend gets released from a mental institution."

I couldn't help but laugh. His sarcasm made me feel weirdly

comfortable. He wasn't indulging me or feeling sorry for me, which was refreshing. I laughed at my own expense.

"Hey, listen—I took the day off, thought I would take you to lunch, maybe talk a bit. How does that sound?"

Oddly enough, it sounded perfect. I knew sitting here alone would only give my brain time to play more unwarranted tricks on me.

"Sure. That sounds great, actually."

Before hopping in the shower, I looked over the bottle sitting on my vanity, almost staring and pleading with me to take the little blue pill inside of it. I walked over to the bottle, opening it, popping the pill into my mouth. The thought did enter my mind: Would Anna come back if I didn't?

Sam spent every second with me, even while I attempted to dress my face with what makeup I had.

"You did miss me, didn't you, boy?" I said as I scratched his head playfully. "This will have to do, Sam," I said as I stood and stared into the mirror. I was pale and undeniably too thin. I looked like an exact replica of someone from the movies who was still locked away in a psych unit.

I sat and waited for Everett, contemplating the upcoming conversation. I aimed to share with him my struggle against the urge to reveal the truth about Brooks to everyone, aware that this might provoke Miles into asserting his authority and having me committed again.

I closed my eyes and sighed before beginning my breathing exercises. The need to drink or use would always haunt me, I supposed. I could feel the nagging desire to drink away this anxiety I had drummed up in my head.

The knock at the door startled Sam and me. He began to wail cheerfully and wag his tail in excitement rather than preparing to attack. I rolled my eyes and laughed to myself, wondering if Sam would really protect me if he needed to.

"Hi, there!" I greeted the door eagerly, oddly excited to see Everett again. Except it wasn't Everett who stood before me as the door swung open.

He wore a half-smile, hands tucked in his pockets. His face, as always, was strikingly handsome with features that seemed divinely crafted. Dark, innocent eyes fixed on me, piercing through to my core.

"Miles," I managed, half-stunned, quickly grabbing Sam to prevent him from rushing to greet our unexpected visitor.

"Were you expecting someone else?" he inquired, tilting his head slightly to the side in that thoughtful way of his.

"Yeah, anyone but you!" I spat out, my tone laced with anger and intensity.

"Dr. Newsome called and asked me to check on you," he explained calmly.

"So that's why you're here?" I shot back, my voice infused with bitterness and a hint of betrayal. "Well, here I am, doing just fine." Leaning against the door, I relied on its solidity as my knees wavered beneath me. The conflicting emotions churned inside me, torn between wanting to push him away and desperately longing to pull him closer, a battle I'd fought repeatedly.

"Not entirely. I was coming over anyway. Can I come in? I'd like to talk," he asked softly.

Chapter **Now**

I NODDED, FINALLY LOOSENING my grip on the door that had been my support. Turning away, I started to walk back inside. He trailed behind, catching my shoulder and spinning me around to meet his gaze. The touch sent a shock through me, though I couldn't discern if it was electrifying or repulsive.

"That day, you remember, the day my grandmother died?" As the words left his mouth, I saw Everett, standing directly behind Miles in the doorway.

I looked past Miles and met eyes with Everett. "Everett," I said surprisingly, although I knew he was coming, but his timing was inconvenient. Miles twisted around quickly, both remaining silent as they examined one another.

I managed to make my way back to the doorway, slinking around Miles like a spy very quietly. "Miles, can you give us a minute please?" Not waiting for him to answer, I closed the door and stood in the hallway with Everett.

He was side-eyeing me, "Everything okay?" he asked suspiciously. He could tell I was shaken and a bit of out sorts.

"Its fine, but, um—do you think we could do lunch another

day?" I was fidgeting, nervous about the situation I was in. I wanted to hear Miles out, but I hated to disappoint Everett.

"Quinn, what's going on? Who is that?"

"No one, I mean, it's Miles. He just came to check on me. I need to talk to him. Please. Do you mind?" I begged for some consideration.

"Miles?" he asked puzzled.

"It's a long story, Everett. I planned on telling you some today. Well, I thought about it. It's complicated, that's all."

"You're talking in circles, Quinn." He stood there, not buying into my petition for space.

"I know. Listen, please go," I begged of him as I tried to inch closer to the door, summoning him to go.

The door opened, Miles standing on the other side. "Is everything okay?"

Everett interfered before I had the chance to answer. "I was just asking her that same question," he blurted out before crossing his hands at his chest, putting his tattoo on display as it played peekaboo with his shirt sleeve. Everett was bigger than Miles, his muscles evident even through his T-shirt. He was intimidating for sure.

Neither of them broke the intense eye contact they held with one another. I suddenly felt like a referee in a boxing match. I could feel the testosterone dripping from each of them.

I waved my hands in the air. "Look, I can't do this right now." I turned my head to Miles. "Just go, we can talk later."

I knew by the conversation with Everett before Miles's intrusion, he wasn't budging. He was all of a sudden protective of me, and I kind of liked it.

Miles slightly nodded his head, almost with sarcasm, as if telling Everett that Everett had won the battle, but he would win the war. He exited quietly towards the elevator, giving Everett a snarky look as he turned away.

Everett and I stood there motionless in the hallway before moving inside. A silent moment to regain composure for us both.

I entered as Everett followed. I closed the door behind me, staring down at the knob, stalling somewhat before turning around to explain to him who that was and what had just taken place. I hadn't decided if I was ready to really plunge into the truth, but his gaze was direct, and strong like direct sunlight blasting my eyes. I couldn't hide from it. He needed me to spill it.

It's now or never, I guess. He had confided his truth in me, here I go.

He sat and listened intently, quiet as I purged the ugly truth. Starting from losing my dad, I sobbed on the sofa, tearing my cuticles to shreds as I shamefully recounted the abuse— the toughest part, more troubling than what we had done to Brooks.

"Everett, say something." He sat at the other end of the couch, eyes lost in thought. He seemed uncertain about what he had gotten himself into.

He opened his mouth, almost speaking but pausing.

"Everett, I know it's a lot." Warm tears dripped from my cheeks onto my chest, quiet to others but thunderous in my ears. Shame poured uncontrollably, eyes betraying my struggle. I tried to halt them, to no avail.

"I don't know what to say. Quinn, this is a lot for one person to go through alone. I only wished you would have shared sooner." Moving closer, he still appeared caught off guard, his face searching for certainty, questioning the truth.

"Look, I understand if you want to run. You don't owe me anything." I was at a loss for words.

"No, I don't. I'm just processing what you just told me. And that guy, that was Miles?" His concern was palpable.

"Yes." I omitted the part where we slept together, knowing it might drive him away. Right now, I needed him with me.

"Are you in danger, Quinn? I mean, with Miles? He killed his dad; he's a loose cannon, capable of beating his own father to death." Standing abruptly, he paced the room.

"I don't know, Everett. I feel like maybe I did lose it, and Anna? I mean, I saw her at the funeral years ago, and then she came to see me, yet they found her body. Did I imagine her then, too?" I buried my head in a pillow on the couch, fighting the urge to scream. My head was now throbbing, and my face stung from all the crying. I could feel Sam nudging my toes hanging from the sofa as he attempted to console me.

My face finally emerged from the pillow. I could see Everett in the kitchen, both hands on the countertop, lost in reason.

"What do I do, Everett?" I was genuinely hoping he had come to a miraculous resolution to make this all go away, or at least make it all right. I would have been alright with either in this moment.

"Honestly, I don't know." He removed his grasp on the counter and made his way back to the couch situating next to me. The look on his face was no longer uncertainty, but sympathy.

His arms wrapped around me gently, and his hands cupped my head as he drew it into his chest.

"We will figure it out, Quinn," he said softly and convincingly. And for the time being, I believed him.

He released his hold of me, looking down at my red-stained cheeks. "Make me a promise," he said.

I sat quietly, anticipating his next sentence.

"Stay away from Miles."

I nodded yes and fell back into his chest once more.

Chapter Now

THE NEXT MORNING, I woke to Sam breathing heavily in my face, all but saying aloud to take him outside to relieve himself. "Fine, Sam," I scolded him as I rubbed my eyes and forced myself out of bed.

I had precisely one hour to dress and leave for my appointment with the new doctor. While getting ready, I reflected on the previous day, especially my conversation with Everett. Not once did I consider having a drink or getting high. *Okay, Quinn, that's progress,* I thought to myself. Speaking of which, I sent Sherry a text: "I'll see you tonight." I had promised her I would return this week, and I intended to keep that promise. I headed out the door and made my way downtown.

The doctor's office was smaller than I expected. There were only two chairs in the waiting room, which was nice. It felt private and intimate, not like any other doctor's office I had ever visited; but of course, I hadn't visited many.

The receptionist was an older woman with short white hair and a welcoming demeanor. "Hello there, honey. You must be Quinn Barlow. Welcome in." I nodded my head yes at her assumption as she handed me a stack of papers. "Now, if you want to take a seat and start filling these out, Dr. Randle will be right with you."

I did as I was told and took a seat. Thankfully, I was the only one in the waiting area, which put my mind at ease. There was no one to judge me or look at me and wonder what I was here for. I was different now, recalling all the times I had no care about what I looked like, sitting in the ER waiting to beg for my next fix. *Quinn, you have made progress.* I silently patted myself on the back as I began to fill out the papers.

As I finished up, the door opened, a middle-aged woman looked at me and smiled. "You must be Quinn. Come on in." She waved me in, and as I passed the receptionist, I handed her my pile of forms and said thank you.

There was only one room, her office. I stood at the doorway looking around before making my way to one of the chairs across from what I assumed was her chair.

She was still standing, gesturing for me to sit first.

I felt some panic pierce my being, dreading revealing my story once again. I felt uncomfortable and fidgety, unable to relax as I sat.

"Hi, Quinn. I am Dr. Randle." Her voice was eloquent, and she immediately reminded me of the receptionist. Their smiles favored along with bright red lipstick.

"Take a seat, please. I assume you filled out all your paperwork with my mother—excuse me, Judy." She delicately laughed as she finished her sentence. "I have downsized, as you can see. I decided that a smaller, more intimate environment was more suitable for my clients."

"You look alike, you and your mother," I inserted quietly.

"What's that?"

"Your mother, you look just like her, I mean a younger version."

"Thank you." She smiled. "I am still working on calling her

Judy, rather than Mom. Speaking of mothers, I have already read your file. Dr. Newsome forwarded it to me."

The apprehension came over me again, and I was unsure if I felt embarrassed or thankful. I knew I would still have to tell my story again, though, so I decided on embarrassed. My face felt like it was turning beet red. It was odd, standing in front of a woman that was so accomplished, with pictures of her accomplishments hung from every wall as I peered around. She was probably about 15 years older than me, but I knew I would never have anything like this to be proud of.

"What is it, Quinn? May I call you Quinn?"

She could feel me gazing around and appearing to feel uneasy, I could tell by the inquisitive look upon her face. I finally sat.

"Please, yes, call me Quinn. Harvard?"

I was staring at an elaborate frame that held one of those fancy degrees that had signatures you couldn't possibly read marked all over it. The only thing that stood out was Harvard.

Her voice softened somewhat as she spoke this time. "I did go to Harvard," she said as she walked over to the frame and gazed at it.

"You know, Quinn, I went to Harvard because my mother worked two jobs and made sure I had every opportunity in the world. I had a different childhood than you." She was looking me straight in the eyes while she spoke. "Quinn, your innocence was taken at an early age, and that isn't your fault."

She had evidently read my file, and she made no qualms jumping right in.

Chapter Now

LEAVING DR. RANDLE's office, I felt a sense of relief and acceptance. She listened as I recounted my history, jotting down notes along the way. Her presence instilled a sense of security in me. I liked her.

I decided today wasn't a waster after all.

My phone rang as I made my way to the parking lot. I answered, "Hello?"

"What about dinner after group? You in?"

"Sure, Sherry, that sounds nice."

Silence filled the line momentarily. "You want me to bring Sam, don't you?" I gave a little silly laugh.

"Yeah, I mean—I called to see how your appointment went, but I also wanted to check in on my dog."

I laughed again, only this time harder.

"I guess he could sit in the car," I said as I debated my statement in my head.

"No, no, don't do that to my dog. I'll come by soon enough and give him a good scratching."

We hung up as I sat in my car, reading my messages I had received during my appointment. Miles had sent me a message asking to see me.

I want to talk, can I come by?

I almost had half a mind to ask him if his wife knew that, as we had not yet had the opportunity to discuss that he had lied to me.

I hesitated before texting him back. Everett had made me promise to stay away from him, but I wanted to hear what he had to say. *Sure, come by tomorrow, I have a meeting tonight.*

He responded almost immediately. *I have to work tomorrow, I will be there late this evening.*

I didn't respond. I left it alone, knowing he would show up regardless. He was obviously desperate to get something out of his system, and I was willing to let him for my own sanity. I needed to hear what he had to say. Maybe he had changed his mind about helping me.

My drive to the Hopeful House felt normal, almost bringing balance or normality to my existence. Sadly, my normal was unlike that of Dr. Randle's beautiful life, but to me, stability and routine were soothing. I was even looking forward to dinner with Sherry after all she had done for me and for Sam.

I managed to silence the thoughts that had been invading my brain for months, the what ifs and the hows. I cranked up my music and rolled down my windows and let the cold breeze hit my face while I sang along to the Eagles.

The group and dinner went well. The fact that there were others out there struggling just as I had disturbingly strengthened me. I don't know why I felt like the meetings were a chore. I always left feeling better than I had gone.

On my way home, I pondered Miles's sudden urgency. I decided he had finally come to his senses and wanted to help me confront the truth about his monstrous father. But as I considered what that meant for me—exposing him to the world, screaming about how he had ruined my life and the lives of others—I found myself tangled in conflicting thoughts. Was

I pursuing this to shift blame away from my own choices? Did I truly seek justice for Brooks's actions, or was it just a desperate need to assign fault? The weight of guilt washed over me like a lingering headache from a night of excess. I needed clarity on my motives—was it closure for Kent's wife, searching for answers about her sister's disappearance, or justice for my mother, whom I believed was murdered by that beast? I wrestled with myself, striving to validate my intentions. The parking lot was desolate when I arrived home, I could see lights on in most apartments, assuming families and couples were cleaning up from the evening and getting ready for bed, a simplicity that I envied.

As I neared the entrance to the building, I felt someone behind me, footsteps inching closer. A hand grabbed my shoulder as I reached for my key.

"Miles, damn it!" I bellowed. "You scared the life out of me. What is it with you, you seem to do that, show up out of nowhere and frighten me? Jesus."

His presence in that moment seemed large, suspended over me under the streetlamp that lit the sidewalk. His shadow engulfed the door that I had now turned to open.

"I didn't mean to scare you. I'm sorry, Quinn." He said as I opened the door, holding it for him as he followed. "I saw you pull up. I didn't want to alarm anyone and holler at you."

"It's fine," I said as I motioned him toward the elevator.

He followed me silently to my door. "Feel free to wait," I said briskly, grabbing Sam's leash. "I won't be long."

$\mathscr{Chapter}$ Now

WHEN SAM AND I returned to my apartment, Miles had made himself comfortable on the couch. His presence made me a bit uneasy, and all I could think about was my promise to Everett. He acted as if Miles was a danger to me, which I hardly believed, but nonetheless I had vowed to him I would.

Sam immediately rushed Miles, only to beg for head scratches, welcoming him to our space without hesitation. "I'm not sure he is indeed suitable as a guard dog, but he's a great companion," I said as I gave a thin smile towards Sam.

I sat across from Miles with my arms crossed across my chest.

"Well?" I finally asked. "Why are you here? What did you want to talk about?"

"The day my grandmother died," he said as he looked at me intensely, never removing his eyes from mine.

"What about it, Miles?" I asked curtly.

"I didn't kill my father, Quinn, but I did add something to her tea. I did that, Quinn." He was now staring at the floor. I could see a single tear roll down his cheek, hitting his scrubs and disappearing.

I instantly released my arms from my chest, inadvertently cupping my mouth momentarily. All those years ago, I had convinced myself he wasn't capable of this, but he was. He did.

"Miles," I said in shock.

"I know." He shook his head. "She was vile, I couldn't take it anymore. I didn't think it would kill her, Quinn. I don't know what I thought." His hands were rubbing his forehead, his temples bulged out from his hairline.

I got up from the couch and moved towards him, sitting right next to him.

"How could you do that, Miles? You killed her. And Kent—what he went through that day, it was traumatizing." Even as I entertained the thought of him removing that despicable woman from this earth, I couldn't deny the sick satisfaction it brought me. Why was he confiding in me now? Was he trying to regain my trust?

"Quinn! Our whole life was traumatizing. I know what I did, I know it was terrible. I just didn't think it would kill her. I really didn't." He had taken my hand; I could feel the heat emanating from his fingers and palms as he clutched mine. I didn't pull away. I let him have a moment, remaining silent as I sorted out what he had said. We sat there quietly for what felt like ages.

"Okay," I finally said.

"Okay?" he repeated.

We sat there, hand in hand on the couch waiting for the other to go on.

I didn't know what to say. He obviously didn't either, only to sit there in another awkward long moment of silence.

He finally spoke, "Quinn. Please. Can you please just move on. My father will never bother you or anyone else ever again. Can't you just move on with your life? We have."

His plea angered me. How easy it had been for them to move on, or so it felt like.

"I don't understand. Move on? What about what he did? To those children? To those families? To me? His reputation in that town—it's repulsive."

He cut me off mid-sentence. "Damn it, Quinn, I'm trying to protect you. It's all I've ever done. It's all Kent ever did! He's dead, damn it!" His voice boomed with intensity and sternness.

I let his hands go, peering at him, trying not to scream back. I could feel my anxiety rising and my body began to stiffen.

He began to speak again, softly this time. "You really don't remember anything, do you?" he said as he stood, making his way over to the mantle. He perched both hands on top of the mantle leaning in as if he were stretching.

He was staring at the floor, intensely displaced in thought.

"How could I forget what happened, Miles? I haven't slept properly in years, constantly remembering what he did to me, that night, and then you running away. What do you mean I don't remember?" Tears streamed down my cheeks, though I wasn't sure why. Dizziness washed over me, and suddenly I craved a drink. My hands clenched, legs restless. I stood and faced Miles at the mantle, waiting for his response. He looked back at me silently. Moving towards the door, he paused as his hand touched the knob.

Before he turned the knob, he stated firmly, "Quinn, you're unwell. I mean it. Please, just move on. It's for your own sake." With that, he opened the door and walked out, never looking back as it slammed shut behind him.

Chapter Now

LIKE MOST NIGHTS, I didn't sleep well. I didn't know what moving on would even look like. *I'll just pretend this never happened. Accept that Anna was a figment of my imagination, a delusional breakdown, and that Brooks would never be held responsible for all those murders, or the abuse and pain he caused me, and my mother. Was I capable?* All I knew for certain was that I was tired. Tired of chasing ghosts and answers. I had a good support system now, and with their help, just maybe I would be capable.

I rolled over to grab my cell phone and call Claudia. I needed something else to concentrate on, to give my head a rest.

"Hey, Claudia," I said as she answered on the second ring.

"Quinn! How are you feeling today?" Claudia's voice sounded genuinely concerned.

"Good, I think," I replied hesitantly with a little laugh to follow. "I'm coming in today, I mean if that's still alright with you?"

"Absolutely, sweetheart," Claudia responded warmly.

"I'll be there in about an hour," I replied before hanging up and stepping into the shower.

As I hopped out of the shower, my phone buzzed. "Hi, there," I answered.

"Good morning," Everett said cheerfully. "How was your night?"

"Had dinner with Sherry after our meeting. It was nice, normal. Felt good."

"Glad to hear that, Quinn. And your doctor's appointment? Also went well, I presume. I never heard back from you."

"I'm sorry, I got your message. It was just a big day, that's all. You snuck out the other night. Didn't tell me goodbye."

"I didn't want to wake you. You needed the rest. Looked like sleeping beauty." He laughed.

"Oh yeah?" I snickered back. "Is that right?"

"No way! You were snoring, that is why I really left. Kept waking me. Sounded like a chainsaw testing factory. I had to get out of there."

We both laughed. He could always make me laugh; I adored his lighthearted jokes.

"Plans for the day?" he asked.

"Actually, yes. I'm going to work today."

"Already? You are sure you're up for that so soon?"

"Yeah, I think so. I'm actually getting ready now. Can I call you tonight?"

"No, but I'll pick you up at seven for dinner."

"See you at seven, then," I said sarcastically, playing into his silly charm of demand.

Making my way to the flower shop felt ironically ordinary but so promising. The sound of Claudia welcoming me in the door was warming and was just what I needed. We bantered back-and-forth as if I had never missed a day. No hugs or tears, only a list of deliveries to prepare. Although she was proud that I was back, the place had made it without me. She had hired a new helper to replace Everett, a young high school student who worked every day after school. I did find myself missing Everett, and our chitchat, but he was now dedicated to his new art studio, and I was proud of him. The world had yet again moved along without me so easily.

The day flew by. I liked the new girl. Sweet and timid, and she didn't talk much, but I didn't mind. I'm sure she would warm up to me soon enough.

"Okay, Claudia, anything else before I head out?"

"No, go on home." She waved me on out the door before pausing, "Hey, sweetie, I'm glad you're back. I missed you."

I blew her a kiss and walked out the door.

It was a little early, as we seemingly were getting more work done faster with less chatter. We had finished our orders over an hour earlier than Everett and I ever did. I blamed it on our flirty antics and maybe dragging it out purposefully to hang out longer with one another.

I decided since I had an extra hour, I would surprise Everett at his new studio. I wanted to see his new space and his work. *Move on.* This was moving on, I persuaded myself. This was what normal people did. They didn't chase down murderers or beg for resolution, they just moved on. So, moving on it was.

The art studio was located approximately half an hour away from the flower shop. With the sun beginning to set in the background, lights illuminated the modern industrial building, perfectly suited for Everett. Everything was just right; he had truly made the most of three months. Self-pity began to creep in once more, reminding me of my inadequacies. Glancing at my watch as I arrived, it read 5:15. The door was heavy, mirrored, and I couldn't see in, but I assumed you could see out. *How fancy*, I thought. As I mustered the strength to pull the door open, I was in awe. The paintings were familiar, and some were of me. My mouth dropped as I made my way in to get a better look. There were people scattered throughout the room, viewing and discussing the artwork. The paintings of me were sad and boldly dark.

It was staggering. I was taken aback temporarily. Is this how he sees me? Sad and broken? As I approached one closer, I read the title: "Beautifully Broken." I stood there, speechless.

"I wasn't ready for you to see this," Everett whispered in my ear.

I didn't know he had caught me sneaking in. I couldn't take my eyes off this particular painting, never looking up to acknowledge his being there.

"Are you upset, Quinn?" he shyly asked.

I turned to him. My cheeks burning with embarrassment or shock, I wasn't sure which. "No, Everett, I'm not upset." I gently kissed his cheek, only to turn back around to admire his work once more. "This is me?"

"Yeah, it's you," he responded quietly as he crept in closer, pressing his body into the back of mine and wrapping his arms around my waist. I looked down at his arms immersing my tiny body, only to see the tattoos that covered his right arm, reminding me that he had overcome so much to get here.

He unlocked his arms from my body. "You're early," he said as I turned back to look at him again.

"Everett, this is amazing. I am so proud of you."

"Well, thank you. I had some inspiration," he said as he smiled at me, brushing his blonde hair aside from his eyes. His hands were now in his pockets. "If you want to hang around and wait on me, you can. I have a few more paintings to show but shouldn't take too long."

"Of course," I said, motioning for him to proceed. "I don't need a babysitter," I quipped, walking off to admire more of his work. He chuckled and headed over to a couple across the room.

Chapter **Now**

I DIDN'T GET TO watch a ton of movies growing up. I was
always busy studying, practicing violin, or sneaking out to
my tree, but I watched some. I remember wondering what
it would feel like to have a fairy tale love, like the kind on tv,
the one where it's just beautiful, and easy, and time seems to
move in slow motion. And although I loved Miles then, it was
complicated then, and I was young. But now I was a grown
woman standing in an art studio with a real man, who I think
loves me for some strange reason. I was frozen there, taking
in that feeling, pretending this was a movie and that I was the
star. Time did stand still right then and there, like a dream.
The paintings were sad and dark, but he saw me and loved me
anyways.

His work was impressive, but most of it went over my
head, highlighting the difference between an artist like him
and someone like me. The abstract paintings he created were
too complex for me to fully grasp. I could only make sense of
the ones featuring me; the rest were interesting but hard to
understand. As I walked around, I found myself respecting
Everett more than when I had first arrived. As I gazed up at
another piece of his work, I heard him come up behind me.

"I sold another!" he exclaimed in excitement. His blue eyes shined with enthusiasm.

"Bravo," I said while mimicking a grand clap to display delight with a touch of sarcasm.

"Let's get out of here and celebrate," he said as he grabbed my hand, pulling me towards the door. "My assistant will close up."

"You've even got yourself an assistant now? Well, Everett, looks like you've made it," I laughed, following him out the door with a sense of pleasure.

Dinner was nice. He talked about his work and his grand opening. I was a bit jealous that I couldn't be there for that; I was instead locked away in a concrete room. The pitch in his voice while he spoke of it was high, beaming sunshine straight from his mouth. I listened as he spoke, noting that usually the conversations revolved around me, and ironically, it was a breath of fresh air to hear him brag a tad.

"What are you thinking about?" he suddenly asked. I caught myself sitting across from him, just watching while he rambled on.

"I'm just listening, that's all. Not thinking of anything but right now." I smiled a shy smile across the table.

"Your doctor appointment, you want to talk about it?"

"No, Everett, I don't," I said, leaning in. "I'm enjoying this right now." Taking a sip from my water, I sat quietly as he pressed on, discussing the upcoming shows he had planned. The night unfolded with a palpable tension between us, electric and undeniable. Standing on my doorstep, bathed in the soft, amber glow of the porch light, Everett and I exchanged a hesitant glance. His hand brushed against mine, sending a shiver down my spine.

With a quiet intensity, he leaned in, his breath warm against my cheek. The air between us crackled with unspoken words and unfulfilled desires. When his lips finally met mine, it was a meeting of broken souls—a gentle exploration that spoke volumes of longing and possibility.

Time seemed to stand still in that fleeting moment, the world outside fading into insignificance.

His kiss was tender yet fervent, pulling me closer with a silent plea for connection. Emotions stirred—desire, uncertainty, and a hint of fear mingled together.

As we reluctantly parted, a heavy silence hung between us, filled with unanswered questions. I closed the door behind me, leaning against it, my heart racing.

Taking a deep breath, I reflected on the significance of that charged moment. "Moving on," I murmured, a bittersweet smile playing on my lips, "sometimes means stepping into the unknown." With newfound resolve, I embraced the uncertainty, aware that this kiss had changed something between us forever.

I slept better than I had in years. My eyes crusted over with a good night's rest. "Good morning, boy," I said as Sam perked up at the first movement of my body, peeking over at me with his big innocent eyes.

I rolled over to check the time on my phone. 7:15 a.m. My phone alerted me of a voicemail from Miles. He had attempted to call me during the night, and I had slept so hard that I never heard it.

Quinn, please call me when you get this. It's important.

I sat up in bed, rubbing my eyes rid of last night's rest, preparing to return Miles's call.

Chapter Now

"Hey," I said as Miles answered my call.

"Quinn, they found him."

"Found him?" I said puzzled. Waiting on him to elaborate.

"Dad, Brooks. They found his body. Kent called."

I immediately jumped from the bed, startling Sam as I did. I began to pace, waiting for him to explain further.

The anxiety took over, that unhinged feeling I used to get when I needed a drink or a fix. My mouth went dry, and my desire persisted. That knotty feeling in my hands made me clench my knuckles, driving my hands into balls, aching my palms.

"Where? What does this mean?"

"Quinn, just please don't do anything drastic. Let me and Kent handle this. Okay?"

"I'm not a damn child!" I shrieked through the phone.

"Please, I'm begging you. Just sit tight for me."

"Sit tight? Or do you mean just keep my mouth shut?"

"Quinn, for Christ's sake!"

He hung up the phone on me before I could go on.

I needed to see Dr. Randle. I was so close to letting it go

like Miles had requested, but the worry and urge was all too
familiar, and so I dialed her number at once.

I called Claudia after hanging up with Dr. Randles' office.
She had told me to come in that morning, and I needed to ask
Claudia for the day off.

On the way to Dr. Randle's office, I thought about the
consequences of our actions. I deliberated internally about
what would happen to us if I told the truth about that night
to the authorities. I tried to tell Kent once, but it was clear he
wasn't going to listen, and it would take more than just going
to Kent.

"Good morning, Quinn," Dr. Randle said as I entered her
office. I had confided in her about the abuse and the suspicions
I had about what Brooks had done to those girls, but I left out
the part about Miles murdering his father in front of me.

"Good morning, I am sorry about this, but I needed to talk
to you."

"Sit. Let's talk."

I was there for what felt like hours, divulging each detail about
what had happened. She listened carefully, rarely interjecting.

"What do I do?" I said as I took a breath and waited for her
to answer. I hadn't realized I had begun crying during my rant.
My face was soaked in tears, and I could feel the heat radiating
from my face.

Dr. Randle paused, looking down at her yellow legal pad
before speaking. "Everything you say in here is confidential."

"I understand that. But what do I do?" I was holding out my
hands in an obvious plea for answers.

"I'm not here to tell you what to do, Quinn. I'm here to help
you work out your feelings and make decisions that are healthy
and responsible." She was so calm, as if I just didn't confess to
being a witness to murder.

"You believe me?" I asked her apprehensively.

"I believe you believe that's what happened."

"So, you don't believe me?" I had stood and was now pacing the hard wood floor. My steps felt heavy, and my mouth was still dry. "I'm going to throw up." I grabbed my stomach and searched for the nearest trash can to vomit in.

While I forced out last night's dinner, Dr. Randle sat in her chair comfortably waiting out my panic attack.

"You're in a safe place right now, Quinn," she reminded me tenderly.

I had instant relief from throwing up. My stomach was no longer turning, and I caught my breath. I began to breathe in and out before sitting back in my chair.

I sat there, reminiscing about how close I had come to transitioning to normal the evening before. Feeling foolish, trusting that I could run away from the past, that I could move on without any resolution. Six was not in the cards for me, and I only thought of Everett and what I had now put him in the middle of.

"I had a visit with Miles, yesterday, Quinn."

"Miles?" I asked. "He came here?"

"Yes. He did. I asked him to."

"Why? Why would you do that?" I questioned.

"Quinn, I think you are dealing with trauma associated dissociation. Your brain is protecting you and has concealed the truth. I can help you."

Chapter Now

D R. RANDLE EXPLAINED to me the definition of what she believed was happening to me.

"I am seeking safety?" I asked.

"The outside world isn't within our control," she explained, "but our inner world is."

Her overwhelming announcement felt like a beating. I was still confused about what she meant by all this, avoiding the actual news she was attempting to convey. I was still focused on my next move and her jargon was confusing me even more.

"I can't listen to this right now. I'm sorry. I have to go," I said with impatience before again hurtling out of my seat for the door.

"I think you should stay. We have more to talk about," she insisted. She was now standing in front of her chair, bargaining for me to sit back down.

I walked out the door, leaving her standing alone in her office.

I wanted to call Everett, tell him they found Brooks and ask for advice, but that meant dragging him in even deeper and I didn't want to be responsible for that sort of havoc in his life. I could call Sherry; she would help me. But again, the guilt

of involving someone else took over. Miles was the only one
I could talk to about this.

Answer my call please. I was tapping the steering wheel as
I drove aimlessly to nowhere.

"Hello."

"Miles."

"Where are you, Quinn?"

"Nowhere. I mean, I went to see Dr. Randle."

"She told you?"

"Told me? What? That you went to see her? Yes, she told me.
Did you tell her the truth about that night? Because she sure
doesn't seem to believe me."

"I did tell her the truth. Quinn, why don't you meet me.
I think you need to hear the truth too."

I didn't have the energy to argue with him and decided to
meet him at a corner café near my house.

The café was deserted. Besides an old couple in a booth in
the corner, we had the place to ourselves.

I waited for Miles to arrive, feeling restless about what this
all meant, having trouble deciphering my reality. After all these
years they had finally found him, but this meant Anna was
never real, she had been a mirage, convincing me he was alive.
My brain had played tricks on me. My head felt woozy as I sat
there in anticipation and disbelief.

I saw him park and make his way to me.

"Hey," he said as he slid into his chair.

He looked fragile and tired as he hunkered down in his seat
before looking up at me.

"Hey," I said back, waiting for him to guide the dialogue.
Nothing has changed I thought, here I am, feeling compassion
for this human whom I loved so deeply at one time. It was
evident he would always have this effect on me. I would never

really be able to move on until I was able to let go of him or what could have been.

"Listen, Quinn, you're not ready to hear what I have to say. I brought you here because I don't want a big scene. So please, don't make one."

"Why would I make a scene? What is happening?" I sat there waiting for an inkling about what was about to be said. Was he angry? Sad? I couldn't tell.

"I went to see Dr. Randle because she asked me to."

"Yeah, I got that," I responded curtly.

"She's good at her job," he said before pausing briefly, "she only needed to have one session with you to call me. We did our internship at the same hospital. We know each other, which I'm assuming is why she called."

"Oh, now I see," I said as I shook my head in frustration.

"See, Quinn? What do you see?" he asked upsettingly.

He draped his hands across the table, almost as if he were reaching in to catch me from a hard fall.

I sat there, angry. Fuming at their conspiracy, feeling somewhat manipulated.

"I didn't kill my father, Quinn. Yes, he died that night. But I am not the one that killed him."

I slammed my fist against the table, "I saw you do it!"

"No, you didn't. Quinn, you killed him."

My body forcefully fled back, and I laughed. It wasn't a happy laugh, a disgusted laugh.

I shook my head in disbelief. "Wow, so you're going to pin this on me? Make me out to be crazy in case I tell someone who actually cares about what really happened? Are you that scared this will ruin your reputation? It was an accident, or at least Brooks was . . . Or are you afraid they'll find out what you did to Frances?"

"I'm not trying to pin anything on you, I'm telling you the truth; I'm trying to protect you."

"I can't believe this is happening." I could feel my blood pressure rising, flushing my being with fury.

"I should've called for help, but that's beside the point now. I didn't kill him—you did. You took that tire iron and kept hitting him, and I tried to stop you, but the rage—I had never seen you like that," he whispered intensely, seated across the table, his gaze fixed on me.

"No." My voice trembled as my mind revisited that night. Flecks of me holding that tire iron invaded my head intrusively.

"I cleaned up and I ran away. I didn't know what to do. I did what I had to do, and I ran."

The anger dissipated and fear took hold of my body. I sat there trying to shake the visions now invading my head.

"Quinn." He paused. "I don't blame you. I wanted to stop him too. After what I did to my grandmother, it could have been me holding that tire iron just as easily. You did what you had to do to survive. We all did."

The waitress's sudden appearance caught us off guard. "Are you ready to order?" she asked, pulling out her pad and pen. We both leaned back, trying to appear composed.

Miles nervously requested more time before dismissing her. "Kent knows. I told him. He knows what happened, Quinn."

I sat there, deliberately remaining quiet, unsure what to say.

"Does he know what he did? I mean, about the girls? About his wife's sister?"

"He does. Why do you think he is trying to help you? He loved our father, but he knows. It's tearing him up. You aren't the only one this affected."

It was flight or fight mode, the realism of my circumstances hitting me in the face like the coldest of winds, taking my breath right from me. The memories hitting my mind like shock therapy. I could remember the night as clear as glass now. In an instant, my whole world had changed. I had buried what I had done so deeply, playing a victim of circumstance for so long.

I held up my hand. "I need a minute, okay?"

He paused momentarily before speaking anyway. "Kent, he is in a tough spot. The truth is . . . I was okay with you not knowing what really happened, but you kept implicating me, Quinn. I had to tell you. I couldn't do this anymore. My brother and I had ten years. Ten years to work through this together, to move on. And well, you—when you were released from prison, you unburied it all. The bodies being discovered, the news—it sent you into a spiral of more delusion. I'm sorry."

He was visibly shaken by his own declaration. I could see misery in his eyes, glassy, fighting back tears. I gave him no choice, and now I was at a loss for words and strength.

"And Quinn, there's more."

Chapter Now

THE WAITRESS CAME back, repeating her question about our readiness to order. I couldn't bring myself to eat; I was teetering on the edge of another panic attack, doing my best to keep it together. I understood why he chose this place—it was quiet, where I couldn't lose control or draw attention. Miles ordered a coffee, simply to satisfy the waitress. This revelation flipped everything upside down for me. Now, I was the one gripping the tire iron, uncertain if I could muster the courage to walk into the police station and confess. I began to question the closure I sought for those girls and their families, feeling a deep sense of shame. The justice and truth I had passionately pursued now seemed hypocritical. Exposing the monster who stole my childhood meant exposing myself. I was torn, unsure which was more unbearable.

"Say something," he urged, his gaze fixed on me from across the table, a peculiar expression crossing his face. I didn't know what to say, so I sat there with my hands submerged in my lap under the table, feeling childlike, waiting for someone to tell me what to say. I was frozen in time, the night replaying like a tape recorder in my head.

"Quinn."

My voice cracked. "You said there's more."

He leaned back in his chair holding a long blink as if he were thinking or preparing to hit me with another blow. He opened his eyes and leaned back in. "Anna, he sent her away. I'm sure you could imagine why."

"No, no, Miles I can't, I can't imagine anything right now. I am in total shock right now. Please just go ahead and tell me."

"Kent figured this out later, after I told him."

"Figured out what later?" My stomach felt queasy once more as I sat slumped in the booth waiting for another sickening surprise.

"Anna was pregnant. He sent her away, paid her off. And when she came back . . ." He paused. "Well, you know what happened." Miles's head dropped in shame as he finished his sentence.

"He killed her," I said with a frail voice, worsening my nausea even further. "And Kent, if he knows, then why not at least place blame on Brooks for the murders of all those girls?"

Miles looked at me confused, his head tilting to the left as if I had just asked him how to cure cancer.

"Quinn? Really. That tarnishes his name, not to mention his own father killed his sister-in-law. It's not that simple. AND it could lead to you." His look had changed, he was looking at me with ignorance and irritation. "The bin of pictures. They're gone, Quinn. I made that decision years ago. You were locked up and I was trying to move on. I'm sorry."

A feeling of defeat rolled throughout my body; the only evidence that could prove my story was gone forever.

"Anna, you said she was pregnant. And sent away . . . please don't tell me he . . . ." I couldn't finish my sentence.

"No. The little boy, he was with some friends of Anna's. Adopted. Kent did some digging."

Miles reached across the table gently grabbing my hand. "I'm sorry."

"Me too," I replied.

"I did see her at the funeral. Anna." Despair washed over me as I thought of her and what she must have suffered at his hands. We sat there in an uncomfortable silence for a moment.

"No, I'm sorry for that night—the night we . . . I shouldn't have. We shouldn't have. I'm married, Quinn, but seeing you . . . it brought back those old feelings, I guess. I loved you."

I shook my head. "Don't apologize. I wanted it. Or at least, I thought I did." Tears welled up, threatening to spill down my cheeks. I sniffled and quickly rubbed my eyes, refusing to let the tears fall.

"I suppose my life is a mess too. I see," he admitted. His confession appeared genuine, yet I couldn't shake the feeling that he was adept at manipulating me. Those sorrowful, dark eyes of his could smooth over any situation effortlessly.

"Miles, what do we do from here?" I asked softly.

"I wish I knew."

Chapter **Now**

MY PHONE WAS buzzing heavily on my ride home from the café, Everett's name displaying across my screen. He was checking in, I was sure. "Hi," I said to him as he answered.

"Hi. How's your day going? How is work?" he asked.

I wanted to scream the truth to him, but I didn't. "Good, and yours?"

"Not bad. Sold a painting this morning," he said with pride.

"Well, that's great news."

"It is. I must paint this evening, but I wanted to call and tell you what a great night I had last night."

"Me too." His words brought peace to my existence, taking my mind back to last night, and watching him smile and chat about his studio softened this morning's news for sure.

"Work? You said it's good today? Lots of deliveries?" he questioned.

"Oh yeah, not too bad. Listen, I'll call you later. Paint good tonight," I said before hurriedly hanging up the phone.

I found myself sitting in the parking lot of the flower shop. The only thing I knew to do was carry on my routine, although hitting up a bar for a drink would really have alleviated some of my anxiety. But I knew better.

Claudia was sitting at the front desk, organizing her receipts. The bell startled her as I entered.

"Quinn? I thought you needed a day off, honey."

"Well, my appointment didn't take as long as I had expected, so here I am, at your service," I said as I gave her my best curtsy.

I needed an Oscar for my brilliant performance, appearing normal as if not to have just found out I was a murderer. *Routine, stick to routine,* I repeated to myself. I didn't know what else to do.

As I headed to the back, Claudia stopped me, "Honey, Everett came by earlier looking for you. He said he wanted to surprise you, take you to lunch or something. You may want to give him a ring, darling," she said as she continued to shuffle through her receipts.

I stopped. "What did you tell him?"

"I told him that you took the day off."

I was still frozen in my tracks. He knew I had lied to him. I continued to the back, my own heart breaking as I made my way to the apron station. That feeling of defeat was nearing once again, the heavy pounding of my shattered chest slashing my insides each time it beat.

Claudia's helper looked up as I finished tying my apron. "Hey there," she spoke as she paused what she was doing. "You, okay?" she asked concerningly. "You're quite pale."

I brushed her off. "Yep, I'm good," I said, waving her off as I slipped an invoice from the board.

Her concern lasted for all of 5 seconds as her phone rang. She answered and became completely distracted by someone on the other line.

I didn't want to face Everett that evening, and I was utterly relieved he had to paint later, giving me more time to scheme up an explanation, leaving Miles out of it. After all, I had taken the day off but just decided to go in. I would figure something out, although it didn't feel good to decide to fib to him. The day once again flew by, and the busy day didn't leave much room for my mind to wander. Grace, Claudia's new help, worked fast and efficiently. I presumed it was her readiness to be done and gone, perhaps to hang with friends or do whatever normal people did these days.

I hurriedly waved goodbye to Claudia, darting out the door before she could inquire about my well-being. Thoughts of my actions raced through my mind as I rushed to my car. Am I the villain, or simply afraid? If I confessed, they would understand—it was justified. He deserved it, I argued with myself as I unlocked my car door. My sense of justice had suddenly become blurred. Not wanting to spend the evening alone, I hurried home to let Sam out. On the way, I decided I would visit Miles's house later. We had left things unresolved, and I needed his help to figure out a plan and ease my mind. Sam was excited to see me as usual. "Hey, buddy," I said exaggeratingly as I scratched his head. We made our way downstairs to the grass below my apartment. The night was chilly, the sun had set, and a few stars made their way through the clouds, reminding me that my dad was up above, probably beating his head against a wall with disappointment. I sat on the bench, unable to think about what could have been had he not passed away. My life would've been so different. I would have him to run to when I needed someone, and maybe even my mother, the small glimpse of tenderness she shared before she went away.

I hated that I couldn't depend on Everett, or that I didn't want to. My life was chaos, and if he knew the truth, what would he say? In some unusual, disturbing way, maybe he would understand? He was responsible for someone losing their life.

He had made a terrible decision with the worst outcome as well. I didn't know, but I wasn't ready to tell him tonight anyhow.

It was surprising what I could uncover on the internet—Miles's home address. I had never visited his place before and felt hesitant. I was concerned his wife, ex-wife, or whatever she was, might be there. I dreaded causing another scene in her presence. She was an unwilling participant, caught up in our troubled history as well. I decided to go anyhow.

Chapter Now

MY PHONE RANG as I clutched the steering wheel, feeling as nervous as the day I was released from prison. Thankfully it was Sherry, my saving grace. Seemed she always had wonderful timing. I needed to hear her voice.

"Hi," I said as I answered my cell.

"How are ya?" she asked. Her voice was raspy, like she'd been crying or sick. I wasn't sure which.

"You don't sound well. You sick?" I asked.

"I have had a darn cold. Nothing worth fretting over, I'm fine. I called to see how you're making it."

"Sam is good, Sherry," I replied as I laughed softly.

"Now, I love that dog, but I really am calling just to check on you." She returned the laugh, coughing after she laughed.

"That is a nasty cough, Sherry." I had taken the phone from my ear as she hacked a few more times.

"Now I am fine, don't you worry about me, but if I'm not feeling up to it this week . . . you may have to run group for me."

I was in no shape to run her group session; I was on the verge of pulling into the nearest corner pub and downing a flight of anything I could get my hands on.

"Sure," I confidently responded. Needing another Oscar for my acting. I only silently urged she would feel up to it by Thursday.

We hung up, agreeing to speak again before Thursday. Miles's house was about 15 minutes from mine. I found it ironic that after all these years we ended up living so close to one another. His home was near the hospital. It made sense, as he was often on call.

It was 7:30, and all the stars were now illuminating the sky. His home was on the end of a cul-de-sac. Only three other homes were in view. I wondered if this was the house he had bought for her. It looked like a home you would raise children in. The yard was landscaped, not a piece of grass out of place, and there was a brick pathway lit with elaborate lighting. It definitely radiated sophistication and money. As I pulled up to the driveway, I suddenly felt a rush of intimidation, the fear making me question my capability of just showing up and knocking on his door unexpectedly. His car was in the driveway, and only his, which eased my mind somewhat.

I mustered up all the courage I had to approach the door. I wasn't sure why I was so nervous, or intimidated, rather. I had known Miles since I was eight years old. I persuaded myself before ringing the doorbell that he was still the same Miles he always had been, and that he had been protecting me, even still.

The doorbell rang, a flashy tone, reminding me of the doorbell from the hell house, loud and obnoxious. The porch light flipped on as the door creaked open slowly.

"Quinn," Miles said, seemingly startled to see me.

"I hope it's alright that I just showed up. After today, with things left unresolved, I really needed someone to talk to. Actually, just to be with." My body language was dreadful, and I could feel my posture hunched over like a child on the porch about to break some bad news about busting out a window with my ball. I was rubbing my hands together, popping my knuckles, waiting for him to open the door wider. His head peered through the small opening.

"How did you know where I live?" he asked almost skeptically. He had yet to open the door fully, his body hiding behind the door.

I stood there silently on the porch, in disarray at his reaction to my presence.

"Is she here?" I finally gathered up the nerve to ask.

"Who?" he said as he slithered his body out the door while closing it behind him. He appeared confused as he asked. He was wearing shorts, no shirt or shoes. His hair was messy, tousled as if he had just worked out. "No, she isn't here. Listen, Quinn, this isn't a good time," he said as he peered back over his shoulder, looking towards the door apprehensively.

"You're right, I should have called. I'm sorry. I just didn't want to be alone." I didn't budge from the porch, hoping that he would have a change of heart and invite me inside.

"I can call you tomorrow. I have some work to do," he uttered impatiently.

As I began to feel my cheeks blush, I saw the blinds move. Someone had peeked through, causing a bright light from inside to surge through to the outside.

"You have company?" I blurted out.

He replied, "No," rather hastily.

"I saw someone, Miles, they just looked through the blinds," I said as I pointed towards the window.

He shook his head in aggravation. "Just go. No one is here. We can talk tomorrow," he repeated.

"I am seeing things again, huh?" I said with frustration. "Making things up in my mind again." I had become irritated, unable to stop my words from flowing. My hands were waving around in the air before I knew it.

Miles glanced around, as though worried his neighbors three acres away might overhear me. "Who's in there?" I asked firmly. "Or should I leave it alone again, Miles? And how many times have you shown up at my house unannounced?" My posture straightened, ready for confrontation. I felt strong and angry, awaiting his response.

"You're right," he said calmly. He knew I was not leaving that house without an answer or some decency at least. He turned around and opened the door, gesturing for me to come inside.

"Dr. Randle?" She was standing in the living area, wearing only a robe.

Chapter Now

I STOOD THERE PUZZLED, waiting for either one of them to start explaining. I looked at Miles. His eyes were dark and scary, not warm and welcoming as they had been only 10 seconds prior. He looked like Brooks. The memory from the evening that Brooks waterboarded me with vodka flashed through my brain, sending a chill up my spine. Neither of them spoke.

"What is going on?" I asked, still feeling stumped.

Dr. Randle looked over at Miles, bidding him to speak.

His face lightened, the muscles around his jaw relaxing. "We were just discussing you," he said suspiciously.

"Discussing me? Without your clothes?" I said as I gave a sarcastic laugh. Nothing was funny and neither one smiled, nor laughed.

"I didn't kill Brooks, did I?" I stood there, astonished by my own breakthrough.

Both suddenly seized stares at one another, then back to me, waiting for me to continue declaring.

I whipped my head around back to Miles. "You piece of shit."

I turned back to Dr. Randle. "Are you really that immoral?"

"Now wait a minute, Quinn," she said as she held up her hand at me, "I've done nothing wrong here."

"You go ahead and tell yourself that if it helps you sleep at night, but you are just as bad as he is." My voice had risen twenty notches as I shouted in rage at her.

Miles had come closer as I was shouting at Dr. Randle, placing his hand on my shoulder before speaking. "Quinn, you're confused. Let's just calm down and talk."

I jerked my shoulder from his hand. "No, you won't sweet talk your way out of this. I want to hear you tell the truth. What happened that night, damn it!" My head began to spin, and I could feel a panic attack drawing closer. "I need water. Can I have water?" I asked as I grabbed my spinning head.

Dr. Randle turned towards the kitchen to fetch me water. She had been there before; she knew exactly where his cups were kept. Miles guided me to the couch, where I struggled against the urge to faint. She returned with a glass of water and a small trash can. I immediately began to vomit in the trash can in front of me.

Dr. Randle wiped my forehead with a rag and guided the water glass to my lips. "This will help," she said softly as I began to sip the water. I could see remnants of something in the bottom of my glass as I drank. I instantly spit the water into the trash can, jumping from the sofa.

"What the hell did you put in my water? Are you trying to drug me!?"

Miles sprung off the couch, grabbing my arm violently. "Drink the damn water, Quinn!" he yelled fiercely back at me, never letting loose my arm. My arm was throbbing from the pressure as I ripped away from his grip.

I burst into tears, looking towards the door looking for my escape route. Dr. Randle was now standing, and I was caught between the two of them.

The crying had turned into forceful sobbing. I snapped at Miles, "You don't love me at all, do you? You slept with me! You were manipulating me, you're just like him!" I was trying to wipe away my tear-soaked face, but they kept rolling down fiercely without wavering.

He moved towards me with weighted steps and struck me across the face without hesitation.

"Miles!" Dr. Randle yelled. "Not like that."

He backed away, but I could see his hands balled into fists resting against his thighs. The slap stung, my face burning with pain and fear.

I wanted to fall to the floor, escape my misery and reality, but I didn't. I darted towards the door, reaching for the doorknob before Miles grabbed my hair, pulling me down to the ground.

Chapter Now

THE FIRST BLOW left me dazed, my head throbbing and vision blurred. Despite Dr. Randle's pleas, Miles's rage knew no bounds. His eyes were filled with malice as he continued to rain blows on me, reminiscent of Brooks's relentless attack. I tried to shield myself with my arms, tasting blood but feeling no pain. Lying there, I thought of Everett standing proudly in his studio. Regret flooded me for not confiding in him, for not sharing where I was going or what I was facing. Here I would die, unable to escape the shadows of my past that had haunted me for so long.

A sudden ringing in my ears was loud, startling me back to existence. Miles fell to the ground beside me, clutching the side of his chest. My vison still fuzzy, I wiped the blood from my eyes to see Kent standing over me holding a gun in his hands, yelling at Dr. Randle to get on the ground. Miles was lying next to me, his eyes open, gasping for air, profusely bleeding from his chest. I couldn't move. I looked at him as he stared back at me, the life fleeing from his eyes. I felt sad for him, only for a moment, remembering how many times he had tried to protect me from the monster, only to become a monster himself.

I woke the next day in a hospital bed, my face covered in bandages.

"You're awake?"

Kent was sitting in a chair he had pulled up next to my bed. His hand was resting on the side of my bed near me, but not touching me.

He pulled it away as I looked at it. "It's okay," I said as I gave him my best attempt at a smile. The bandages were tight, and the attempt at a smile had sent a small pain through my jaw.

"Quinn, your face has taken quite a beating," he said softly, as I delicately held my throbbing jaw.

"That explains it," I softly muttered.

Kent gave me a gentle rub on the arm. "Quinn, I'm sorry."

"You saved my life." It hurt to speak but I pushed through, I was glad he was there when I woke.

"The autopsy, on my dad..." He paused, "Brooks. You couldn't have done that damage, Quinn. There was no way. I went to confront Miles. All this time." He was shaking his head.

I knew Miles had manipulated him, just as he did everyone else in his life. He was just like his dad; the thought made me sad.

"No, I mean—I am sorry for what you went through as a child. What my father did to you. Nora is having the baby next week, and I want you to know I am nothing like my father. It took me a long time to accept the truth." He paused again as his eyes watered. "And I'm sorry for that night on my porch."

I turned my head to catch a glimpse of Nora in the window outside my door.

"Does she know what happened?"

"She does."

He looked down at the bed, then looked back up at me. "She's okay. She wanted to come; she was worried about you.

Quinn, everyone knows. I made sure you got that justice you have been looking for. It's over."

I reached out my hand. "Thank you. And I forgive you."

He smiled, and the tear disappeared from his eye. "You know, I handed in my resignation this morning."

"I know this is tough for you." I looked over at Nora again before continuing. "I know you loved your brother and your father, but you have your own family now."

"Yeah, I loved them, but that's the thing about love, it just changes. You just figure it out along the way, and it grows, and the definition of love—it changes." He looked back down at the floor. "He almost killed you; he would have. He was the sick one, Quinn. I did what I had to do. You know I would have never thought twice about doing it for Nora, for my baby girl. And I would do it again for you."

We sat there quietly, coming to a silent understanding of all that had happened.

I finally broke the silence. "Has anyone else come to see me?" I asked. I wondered if Everett knew what had happened to me.

"Yeah, he's here, Quinn. I wanted to see you first." He stood up and straightened out his slacks before moving towards the door. "You're going to be alright," he said before opening the door to walk out.

Before Kent disappeared from the doorway, Nora peeked in, giving me a gracious smile before grabbing Kent's hand and leading him away, brushing shoulders with Everett as he entered.

He remained silent as he approached my bed. "Come on, there's something we have to take care of," he said softly, pulling the covers off me and gesturing for me to follow him. I sat on the edge of the bed, considering whether to get up and follow. Despite my sore body, the expression on his face compelled me. Adjusting my hospital gown and carefully removing my

IV, I slipped away down the hallway and out to the car. Everett drove in silence. I didn't ask him about our destination; instead, I watched the trees pass by, aware of our route. We were headed to Beaufort, though I wasn't sure why. We arrived at the house, the place that had held me captive for years. He got out of the car and then opened my door. From the trunk, he retrieved a gas can and handed me a box of matches. "We have Kent's blessing. Strike the match, Quinn. It's over."

Made in the USA
Coppell, TX
21 September 2024

37539063R00154